Angel Face

"Name: Catherine Lucas. Age: fourteen and a half. Place: London, England," Jo-Jo recited solemnly. "This chick needs help, but so far she ain't been playing ball, know what I mean? We figured a Guardian of her own age might stand a better chance of helping her sort her life out, right?"

"Right," I replied, grinning from ear to ear. Not only was I being sent back down to earth, but I was going to be hanging around helping out a girl. Awesome.

ANGEL FACE

NARINDER DHAMI

Lions
An Imprint of HarperCollins Publishers

Angel Face was first published in
Great Britain in Lions in 1995

1 3 5 7 9 10 8 6 4 2

Lions is an imprint of HarperCollins Children's Books,
a division of HarperCollins Publishers Ltd, 77-85 Fulham Palace Road,
Hammersmith, London W6 8JB

Copyright © Narinder Dhami 1995

ISBN 0 00 675021 4

The author asserts the moral right to be identified
as the author of the work.

Printed and bound in Great Britain
by HarperCollins Manufacturing Ltd, Glasgow

CHAPTER ONE

I guess if I was honest, I'd have to say that being dead is no big deal. Once you've got over the shock of it, I mean. Problem is, there's not a lot to do Up Here, so you get plenty of time to sit around brooding about what your life might have been like if you hadn't kicked it. We're not supposed to sit around brooding though. We're supposed to sit around looking beatific. Beatific? Real happy, dead joyous, blissed out. I haven't been here long, so I'm not too hot at looking beatific yet, but I'm working on it. Y'know, just between you and me, I can't help wondering if death would have been a bit more exciting Down There.

Sure there's plenty of people to talk to Up Here, and it can be kinda interesting, but it's no way how live people think it's going to be. Live people, LPs, think that as soon as they arrive, they're gonna get to shake James Dean's hand, and tell JFK what a great president he would have been if he hadn't gotten himself shot.

Forget it. I've been Here three months, and I haven't seen one famous person yet. Once I thought I saw Elvis Presley in the distance, and I dashed right on over there to ask him if he was really dead, or just having us all on. I never did find out though. He disappeared behind a cloud before I could get close enough.

I'm still unsure about why I ended up Up Here instead of Down There. I guess it wasn't because I was real holy or saint-like, because I wasn't. I guess it was just that I hadn't done anything really rough in the almost-fifteen years I was alive. I hadn't done drugs, I hadn't gotten a girl pregnant, I hadn't stolen anything (well, only a candy bar from a drugstore when I was eight). Nope, I had just been an all-round, clean-cut American teenager, obsessed with girls, grades, girls and cars. Girls especially.

That morning three months ago when I arrived Up Here was a normal kind of morning. No premonitions, no shivers down the spine, no morbid feelings. Picture the scene. A typical kitchen in Middle America, checked curtains at the window, sun shining, freshly squeezed orange juice, all that happy-family-round-the-breakfast-table-type-thing. Pain In The Rear End (Junior bro) and Pest of the Year (Junior sis) arguing over the plastic Ferrari out of the cereal box, Mom burning the toast and cussing, Dad reading the newspaper. And in between burning and reading, the ancients were getting down to what they did best. Hassling their first-born.

"Your grades are down again, Aidan." Cue accusing look, tinged with just a hint of parental disappointment from Dad over the top of the newspaper. "You and I are going to have a serious talk tonight, son."

"If you thought less about *girls*, Aidan, and more about your *studies*, you'd get on a whole lot better."

Loud aside from Mom, desperately scraping mountains of charcoal into the sink: "Susan! If you spit in Buster's milk once more, I'll make sure you don't sit down for a week."

OK, so Mom and Dad had me nailed. My grades *were* down, and the reason *was* because my priorities were, in order of decreasing importance, a) Girls, by a short head from b) Sport, followed a long way behind by c) Study. Well, if babes are gonna crowd round a tall, dark-haired guy with big blue eyes and long legs, who's not only a brilliant swimmer and a junior diving champion, but also pretty damn ace at basketball, I'm not gonna, like, cramp their style, am I?

"Quit hassling, OK?" I'd mumbled irritably into my cereal. "Anyway, I split up with Shelley last week. I haven't even got a girlfriend at the moment." Obviously I didn't let on that I had my eye on Angie Moreno, and that I was just leaving her to sweat it out for a bit before I finally asked her for a date.

"Ah, yes, Shelley." Cue accusing look number two from Dad. "That girl left eleven messages for you on the answerphone yesterday."

"Only eleven, huh? That's one less than the day before. She must finally be going off me."

"This is serious, Aidan." A beady-eyed glare from Mom. She and Dad had this taking-turns-at-hassling-type-thing down to a fine art. "The poor girl's obviously very upset that you're not dating any more."

"Yeah…" I hadn't finished with Shelley Markowitz because I'd gone off her. I mean, you don't go off blonde hair, long, slim legs and a great personality just like that. No, she'd started getting too clingy, and I'd run a mile. It wasn't like we were married or anything, for God's sake. "I'll have a word with her at school today."

"Do that." Dad had fixed me with a heavy, man-to-man stare as I stood up. "We can't have the answerphone blocked up with pathetic calls from your ex-girlfriends –"

"I said I'll have a word with her," I'd snapped, grabbing my books and slouching over to the door. "OK?"

It wasn't gonna be easy though, I reflected as I slammed the door shut behind me in traditional, teen-rebel style. Shelley just didn't want to be finished with. She was pursuing me relentlessly day and night, in the hope that I'd change my mind and take her back, and the whole affair was rapidly turning into a Fatal-Attraction-type-thing. I could see myself coming home one day to find Buster's pet hamster merrily boiling away in a pan on the stove.

It was because I was thinking about Shelley and my grades and Angie Moreno that I didn't notice the car when I stepped off the sidewalk. And that was it. One minute I was there, the next minute I was Here. No time to say sorry, no time for goodbyes, no time to tell Mom and Dad and Buster and Susan that I loved them - but I don't let myself think about my family too much. If I do, I have big problems looking beatific.

I guess someone must have complained about me not looking beatific enough because I got a message that Jo-Jo wanted to see me. Jo-Jo's kinda looking after me at the moment. Everybody who's just arrived gets a sort of guide to help them settle in, and Jo-Jo's mine. For what it's worth. He was a hippy in the sixties, so he's pretty damn good at sitting around looking blissed out all the time. He kicked it in 1972, a brain tumour or something. Anyway, he's not a bad dude, I guess. Just a bit weird. Your average hippy, basically.

Anyway, I went off to see him, prepared to argue my case. He was looking blissed out as usual, sitting cross-legged in the lotus position. And that ain't easy in these robes, let me tell you.

"Hey, Jo-Jo. Sorry about this, OK? I'm practising my beatific look real hard – it's just taking a while to get it right."

"No sweat, man. That's not what I wanted to see you about." Jo-Jo squinted up at me. "But, hey, you're right. You look more horrific than beatific. It won't do, man. It just won't do."

"So what do you want to see me about then?" I asked, alarmed. Maybe the guy on the gate had made a mistake with the guest list, and I really should have ended up Down There instead of Up Here. I shivered. Hey, I'd only been joking about things being a bit livelier in the Other Place. I hadn't really meant it.

"Give me a minute, man, give me a minute." Jo-Jo stared up at me thoughtfully. He stared at me for so long without saying a word that I began to feel uncomfortable. I knew from experience though that there was no point in trying to hustle him, so I waited.

"It's a problem, man, know what I mean?" Jo-Jo shook his head. "It's, like, a problem."

"What is?"

"This is."

I took a deep breath and gritted my teeth.

"What problem is that then?"

"The problem I'm thinking about right now, man." Jo-Jo untangled his legs and stood up. I briefly considered punching him on the nose, and then remembered where I was.

"So what exactly is the problem you're thinking about right now, Jo-Jo?"

"Give me some space, man. I'm getting there, I'm getting there." He adjusted his headband and nodded at me. "You, man. You're the problem."

"Me?" I swallowed hard. "What have I done?"

"Nothing yet."

"OK, now we're getting somewhere," I

muttered under my breath. "So why am I a problem?"

Jo-Jo looked worried.

"Because it's never been done before, man, dig?"

"What's never been done before?"

"Sending a novice back to Earth as a Guardian Angel. It's like heavy."

"Wh-a-a-at?" My jaw hit my chest. "You talkin' about me?"

"Sure thing, man." Jo-Jo stared at me hard. "We have to be sure you can, like, handle it. That you ain't gonna freak."

"Handle it? 'Course I can handle it! And I won't freak," I gabbled breathlessly, secretly freaking like mad inside. Access to Earth was strictly limited except for Guardian Angels. They kinda beamed down invisibly every so often to give you folks on good ol' Planet Earth a helping hand. But the thing was, they were usually dudes who'd been Up Here for ages. Hey, I'd expected to be around for about five hundred years or so before I was given the chance. Now, after just three months, I could be headed right back where I started from. I could visit my family and friends. Go back to girls, hamburgers, cars, girls, TV and girls. Wow. I looked more beatific than I'd ever done for the whole of the last three months. I was in heaven (if you know what I mean).

"Yeah, this is heavy, man," said Jo-Jo thoughtfully. "But there's this, like, problem, and you're kind of our last hope."

"I am?" I said, with a big grin stretching right across my face. Well, whaddya know?

"Yeah..." Jo-Jo started pacing up and down, looking worried. "The trouble is, y'see, GAs have got to be *subtle*. They've got to know when to butt in, and when to butt out. They've got to give a helping hand when it's needed, but they've got to stay, like, in the background, dig?" He looked me up and down, sighed and shook his head. "And frankly, Aidan my man, you just don't look like an in-the-background sort of guy."

"Oh, I am, I am!" I promised recklessly. "Whatever you want, I can do it." I'd promise just about anything if it only got me back down to earth for a while.

"Cool it, man," Jo-Jo said quickly. "We ain't made up our minds if you're the right dude for the job yet."

"Jo-Jo, believe me, I am," I said urgently. Hey, I didn't know what the job *was* yet, but I didn't even care. Getting myself back down to earth quick-smart was the important thing here.

I mean, it's pretty blissful and all that Up Here, but you need time to settle in. And when you were whisked off the face of the earth and Up Here in precisely ten seconds flat like I was, you can't help missing what you left behind just a bit. "What's the story?"

"Name: Catherine Lucas. Age: fourteen and a half. Place: London, England," Jo-Jo recited solemnly. "This chick needs help, but so far she ain't been playing ball, know what I mean? We figured a Guardian of her own age might stand a better chance of helping her sort her life out, right?"

"Right," I replied, grinning from ear to ear. Not only was I being sent back down to earth, but I was going to be hanging around helping out a girl. Awesome.

"Trust me, Jo-Jo." I stopped grinning, and tried to look stern and trustworthy and kinda Guardian Angelish. "Babes – I mean, girls – are my number one speciality. I can handle this thing. No sweat, man."

CHAPTER TWO

I made it back down to earth about as fast as I'd
left it three months ago. One second Jo-Jo was
flapping on about what I was expected to do,
and the next second there was a blinding flash
of light, and I was standing in the middle of a
busy street. Hey, I'd been expecting a fanfare of
trumpets, or a formal goodbye-and-good-luck
ceremony or *something*. For a moment or two I
was in a complete daze. There were cars and
buses roaring up and down the road, and people
everywhere. After the peace and quiet Up
There, the noise and confusion was deafening. I
panicked.

"Cool it, man!" Jo-Jo hissed in my ear. I
leapt five feet in the air and looked behind me.
There was no one there. "I told you," – the
voice from nowhere went on – "they can't see
you. You're invisible."

"Where are you?" I stammered, looking
around me nervously.

"I ain't allowed to come with you, but it's

cool – I'll be in constant touch." There was a snappy edge to Jo-Jo's voice that I hadn't heard before. "I told you all this once, Aidan, man. Can it be that you weren't, like, listening?"

I didn't answer. I was totally overwhelmed. I was back on earth. For real. Real shops, real cars, live people. London, England. I'd never been to England before, but it didn't look a whole lot different to my old home town. Somewhere in the U.S. of A. thousands of miles away, Mom, Dad, Buster and Susan would be at work and at school, living out their daily routine, not knowing I was back... I blinked away the hot tears that suddenly scalded my eyes.

"I'm back," I said softly, staring at the world going about its business around me. "I'm really, really back." And it felt like I'd never even been away...

"OK, man, let's get this show on the road. The school's right behind you."

"What?" I jumped as Jo-Jo hissed in my ear. "What school?"

"Hey, Petersfield Comprehensive. Catherine's school."

"Oh. Yeah," I said absently. A woman with a dog on a lead seemed to be walking straight towards me, and I moved hastily out of her way. "You sure I'm invisible?"

"Hey, man, get real." Jo-Jo was beginning to sound distinctly unthrilled. "Now haul your backside into school, find Catherine Lucas and let's get this show on the road. She's in Room 108."

"OK, OK. Just chill out for a minute, will you?" I'd noticed a pretty, dark-haired girl running down the street towards me, and I quickly moved sideways, deliberately blocking her path. Her expression didn't change, and she didn't stop. She simply ran straight through me, and out the other side. I'm telling you, it was a weird sensation. "Hey, I really am invisible!"

"Yeah. Like I told you."

"This is awesome!" Grinning from ear to ear, I stepped off the sidewalk, and into the path of a red sports car that was zooming up the road. The car whooshed straight through me so fast, it sent me spinning round like a top.

"Dirtbrain!" I yelled furiously.

"Man, if you don't get your butt into that building in the next ten seconds –" the normally mellowed-out Jo-Jo was starting to sound just a tiny bit dangerous "– there's gonna be some really bad vibes round here."

"OK, OK, I'm going." For the first time I took a good look at the school. It was just an ordinary red-brick building, nothing special.

Reluctantly I slouched through the gate, heaving a silent sigh of frustration. I could think of a whole heap of things I'd rather be doing now that I'd finally made it back to earth, and trailing round a boring old school wasn't one of them. Still, had to keep the Boss Man happy…

The smell of school – chalkdust, old socks and chemical experiments – hit me in the face as I walked down the main corridor. It reminded me of my school back home, and I had to gulp down a strangely large lump that rose in my throat. Worst of all, I turned a corner, and came face to face with a poster of the old Stars and Stripes pinned to a noticeboard with a message underneath: "Our American exchange students arrive soon, and we need to find places for them to stay. If you and your family can help, please see Mr. Walker." As I stared at the red, white and blue, I had to blink fiercely to stop my eyes blurring. Concentrate, Aidan. Room 108, and the girl whose life I was here to transform, Catherine Whatever-her-name-was.

The school was on three levels, and Room 108 was on the top floor. As I went upstairs, I passed a couple of teachers going down. One was a man in a tweed jacket (original, huh?) and the other was a woman with a face like a warthog.

"Hi." I gave them a friendly wave. "I always thought all teachers suck, and you two are the worst pair of dorks I've ever seen."

"Quit foolin'!" That was Jo-Jo again, loud and clear. This constant nagging was starting to get me down somewhat seriously. "Just stay on the job, and cut the fancy bits."

I found Room 108 without any hassles, and stood on my toes so that I could look through the window. A crone with a hairstyle set in concrete was sitting at a desk at the front of the room, grading essays. The class of about thirty kids was working in complete silence, heads bent over their books.

"Get on with it, man."

"What? Go in there, you mean?" I asked fearfully. "I can't. What about the old witch at the front?"

"They can't see you, they can't hear you, remember? Now are you going to go through that door on your own, man, or do I have to give you a shove?"

"What happened to peace, love and understanding?" I gibed sulkily as I stalked through the door (and through is right). As soon as I was inside the room, I froze nervously, waiting for somebody to notice me and scream or faint. But nobody did. They didn't even know I was there. It felt ultra-weird. This being-invisible-type-thing sure took a lot of getting used to.

"The chick, Catherine Lucas," Jo-Jo whispered in my ear, "she's –"

"Hey, don't tell me which one she is, OK? Let me guess." I scanned the room with the skilled eye of the practised teenage flirt. There were about seventeen girls sitting there, and at least eight were worthy of closer attention. I decided to start with the best-looking babe there.

"Is it that dark-haired girl in the corner?" I asked hopefully.

"Nah."

"Ummm... The little redhead with the cute nose?"

"This is wasting time, man. Why don't I just tell you?"

"Because it's more fun this way, Jo-Jo. Remember fun?" I sauntered up an aisle between two rows of desks, checking out the girls who sat on either side. I was beginning to enjoy myself. This invisibility thing had distinct possibilities.

"...and so I told her to bog off. I mean, who the hell does Catherine Lucas think she is, anyway?"

I spun round, ears flapping. Two girls, a pretty cool blonde and a not half bad brunette, were whispering to each other behind tattered copies of *Macbeth*. I moved closer to them.

"Don't take any notice of her," whispered the brunette. "Nobody likes her anyway."

"Yeah, and it's not hard to see why, is it?" snapped the blonde. "She's only a swot - and a flamin' ugly one at that."

"Yeah, well, she can't help being a dog," said the brunette generously.

"No, but she doesn't have to be so rude and obnoxious with it, does she?"

"Jo-Jo," I stammered faintly as the two girls bent over their work again. "Which - which one is Catherine Lucas?"

"Hey, I thought you wanted to work that one out for yourself?"

"Not any more. Just tell me."

"Hey, didn't you say it would be more groovy to guess?"

"Just tell me, OK?" I snapped furiously. I was beginning to feel that perhaps I'd bitten off more than I could chew here.

"Cool it, man. No need to shout. That chick over there. The one sitting on her own. That's Catherine."

I turned, I looked and I nearly collapsed.

Catherine Lucas was sitting alone in a corner, shoulders hunched over her desk. She was wearing an old jumper with holes in the elbows, and a skirt that didn't fit properly. She had lank, greasy hair, a faceful of zits and a permanent frown. A monster. Godzilla in female form. I turned white. Help.

"Hey, er, Jo-Jo," I murmured faintly. "You were right. I guess I'm not quite up to this thing after all. Maybe somebody with a bit more experience should be sorting out this loser, I mean, this poor unfortunate girl."

"Hey, Aidan, don't badmouth yourself, man." Although I couldn't see Jo-Jo, it sounded to me like he was grinning his stupid hippy head off. "You can handle this thing. No sweat, man."

CHAPTER THREE

Terrific. Totally terrific. I'd been so keen to get back down to earth, I hadn't realised I was supposed to wade in and help out the Schoolgirl from Horrorville. This female (if you could call her that) was positively and definitely beyond all help. Now the only thing I could think of was getting myself taken off the case.

"Yeah, but Jo-Jo, look at it this way." I was standing at the school gates, waiting for the home buzzer to go. I was supposed to wait for Catherine (Zit-Face) Lucas and follow her home. First time ever in my whole life that I'd hung around the school gates waiting for a greasy-haired female with the personal charisma of a cockroach. "I mean, that babe's a lost cause."

"Wrong, Aidan," said Jo-Jo softly. "No-one's ever a lost cause to us. That's why we're Up Here, instead of Down There…"

"Sure," I agreed hastily. That had sounded ever so slightly like a veiled threat. "Er, I'll be glad to hang around and give the girl a hand." A sudden thought struck me. "Um, Jo-Jo? What exactly is it I'm supposed to be doing here?"

"You'll find out more when you follow Catherine home," Jo-Jo said sternly. "Just remember what I told you about a Guardian Angel's duties, man, and you'll be fine."

It sounded like a breeze. I don't think. So I was well and truly in it up to my neck, I thought dismally as the home buzzer sounded in the distance. Even the thrill of returning to earth had faded a bit now that I was faced with the uphill task of transforming Greaseball Lucas's life. I mean, even the Boss Man himself would've had problems with this one.

Doors were crashing open all round the school now, and streams of kids were pouring out into the grounds. I blinked. All of a sudden, there were girls everywhere. Dark-haired girls, blonde girls, slim girls, curvy girls, tall girls, short girls. My eyes lit up like neon signs.

"Remember, man, there's only one chick you're interested in." That was Jo-Jo, sticking his nose in again where it sure wasn't required. "Here she comes now."

I gulped. Catherine Lucas, greasy head down, was shuffling her way out of the door. She looked about a million times worse in strong daylight.

"I feel sick," I said faintly.

"Don't be a weakling, man."

I forced myself to watch Catherine as she walked over to the gate where I was standing. She didn't speak to anyone, and no one spoke to her. Nobody even said, "See you tomorrow." Nobody said a word. I couldn't help feeling a bit sorry for her, but it also confirmed my previous suspicion that she was such a dork, nobody liked her.

"I'm supposed to go with her, right?" I muttered reluctantly as Catherine went past me and out of the gate. I noticed that she had holes in both legs of her pantyhose.

"Yeah, that's the deal. Move it."

I had to sprint after Catherine to catch her up. She was half-running, half-walking, and generally moving along the sidewalk at a pretty speedy pace.

"What's she in such a hurry for?" I complained breathlessly to Jo-Jo. "Has she got a bus to catch or something?"

"No bus, man. Just keep up with her."

Forty minutes and two and a half miles later, I was distinctly unthrilled. The Lucas was still charging on ahead of me like a demented bull, and I was racing along, trying not to get left behind. I didn't even have time to check out the scenery or the girls, we were travelling so fast.

"Hey, Jo-Jo," I wheezed. "How much further to her house?"

"Another few minutes or so, man. That's all."

"I don't get it," I grumbled. "You mean this babe walks an hour and twenty minutes every day to get to school and back? She must be nutsoid! How come she doesn't take the bus like a normal human being?"

"She's trying to save bread, man."

"Save bread, I mean, money? What for?" I put on a spurt to follow The Lucas round a corner. "Plastic surgery?"

"You'll see, man, you'll see. Here, this is her pad."

Catherine's pad – apologies, house – was like Lucas herself. A major mess. The tiny front garden was a mass of weeds, the gate was hanging off its hinges and the whole house looked as though it was about to self-destruct.

"She lives *here*?" I hissed incredulously as Catherine went up the path to the front door. "What a lousy dump…"

I broke off as Lucas unlocked the door, and pushed it wide open. A dark-haired woman in a wheelchair was rolling herself down the hallway towards us.

"Is that you, love?"

"Hello, Mum." As Catherine closed the door behind her, I saw her face light up into a smile, the first one I'd seen all day. "How are you feeling?"

I stood alone in the overgrown garden, feeling dazed.

"That's her mom, right, Jo-Jo?"

"Right, brainbox."

"What's the matter with her?"

"She's got a muscle disease, man. She can't walk."

I ran my hand through my hair, trying to make sense of what I was hearing.

"What about Catherine's dad?"

"Divorced, and living abroad. They don't see him. You'd better get in there, man."

Frowning, I slipped through the door. I was at last beginning to realize why Catherine Lucas needed a Guardian Angel so badly. As I materialized in the hallway, I had a good look round. It was clean enough, but shabby, with peeling wallpaper and old, cracked paintwork. It was also freezing cold.

The sound of a television was coming from behind a door on my right, so I went through. Catherine's mom was sitting in her wheelchair in front of an electric fire, watching a quiz show. Apart from the TV, there was nothing in the room except two lumpy-looking armchairs, a threadbare carpet and a bed.

"Jeez," I muttered, shocked. "What's going on here? This is like something out of Charles Dickens."

"Like I said, man," Jo-Jo said softly and sadly in my ear. "No bread."

The kitchen, the only other room downstairs, was even worse. It was dark, cramped and smelly, and everything in there looked circa 1940. I was shocked. I didn't realize that people in the free Western world had kitchens like that any more.

Catherine was standing near the sink, her back to me, and I looked over her shoulder. She was slicing bread and cheese and tomatoes, and putting them under a hot grill to toast. Chewing at my bottom lip, I paced up and down the tiny room, feeling more and more uncomfortable. Bread and cheese. Was that all they were going to eat tonight?

"What's the rest of the house like?" I asked Jo-Jo urgently.

"Take a look, man."

I gave myself a quick, guided tour. It was bad. The whole place was falling apart somewhat seriously, and, except for the lounge where Catherine's mom seemed to spend all her time, it was like an ice-box. The worst place was Catherine's bedroom. It had nothing in it, except for a bed and a clothes closet. No posters on the wall, no cosmetics lying around, no records, tapes or CDs – nothing. As I stood there in the middle of that cold, depressing dump, I couldn't help thinking of my old bedroom back home. Large, sunny, plastered with posters, a computer, a telephone, a hi-fi system, all my swimming medals and diving trophies... I shook my head sadly. Yeah, I was certainly feeling more and more sorry for Catherine, but at the same time, I was also becoming more and more convinced that I was totally the wrong dude for this job.

I went downstairs. Catherine and her mom were sitting in the lounge in front of the TV, eating bread and cheese off cracked plates.

"Hey, Jo-Jo," I said angrily. "This is seriously dire. I mean, it's sick. There's got to be something somebody can do."

"Catherine won't tell anybody what's goin' on, man. That's why you're here."

I shook my head.

"This is too radical for me," I hissed urgently. "What about welfare, or whatever they call it over here?"

"Social Services, man. And Catherine won't ask for help."

"Charities for the disabled, then. There's got to be something."

"Catherine doesn't want charity. The chick's got her pride," Jo-Jo said sadly. "Like I said, Aidan my friend, that's why you're here."

"But –"

"Have you got any homework tonight, love?" I bit back my reply to listen to what Catherine and her mom were saying. But I wasn't finished with Jo-Jo yet. Not by a long way. I was outta here as soon as I could fix it.

"No, I did most of it at school today. I've just got an essay to finish off." Catherine got to her feet and picked up the empty plates. "I'll do it when I get back." She glanced at the cheap watch on her wrist. "I'll have to go up and change or I'll be late."

"Hey, Jo-Jo," I said, puzzled, as Catherine left the room. "Where's she going now?"

"Didn't I mention it, man? She's got a part-time job at the Bigshot Burger Bar in town."

"You're kidding me!"

"I kid you not, man. She works three nights in the week, and all day Saturday. Like I said…"

"No bread," I finished the sentence for him, my mind in a whirl. I sat down in the armchair

Catherine had just vacated and closed my eyes. This was serious stuff here. I was in way, way over my head.

"I'll be off then, Mum." Catherine hurried back into the living-room. She'd changed into a gross red and white checked dress with a stupid frilly apron, and she had a frilly cap in her hand. "I'm late as it is."

"Take care, love." Her mom hugged Catherine as she bent over to kiss her. A big lump rose in my throat for no reason whatsoever, and I coughed hastily to clear it. "Oh, I wish you didn't have to do this. It's not right at your age."

"Mum, I'm fine," Catherine interrupted her impatiently. It seemed to be a conversation they'd had a few times before. "See you about ten-thirty."

"She works until ten-thirty?" I repeated, horrified, as I tailed Catherine out of the house. "And then she gets up and goes to school next day?"

"Yep. She needs help, like, badly, man."

"Yeah, but Jo-Jo, I don't think I'm the right person to give it," I broke in desperately as I sprinted after Lucas, who'd gone whizzing off down the street again at top speed. "I just don't see what I can do."

"Sure. We hear what you're saying, man," Jo-Jo interrupted soothingly. "But we kinda hoped that you might be able to work on Catherine a bit. Make her see that she needs some outside help."

"How?" I muttered through my teeth. "I mean, I'm not even allowed to speak to the girl, am I?"

"Nope, but I told you how GAs operate. And we thought you might stand a chance, you being the same sorta age, and a hit with the chicks, so to speak."

"I can't do this thing, Jo-Jo," I said, beginning to panic. "I just can't. I'll screw up. I know I will."

There was a long silence. I followed Catherine across a busy road, and a guy on a motorbike went straight through me. I hardly even noticed. I was too busy worrying about what would happen if the Boss Man wouldn't let me go back Up There right now.

"Jo-Jo? You still there?"

"Yeah, man." There was a loud sigh in my ear. "I've been thinking over what you laid on me, and you're right. It was a real stupid idea from the start."

"So I'm off the case?" I asked eagerly.

"Not till we sort out a replacement, man."

Jo-Jo's voice was getting fainter, and I had to strain my ears to hear him. "I've got to go and get this thing straight. Can you stay cool without me for a while? I'll be in touch."

"Sure." I didn't add that not having him droning on in my ear for a bit would allow me to enjoy the short time I had left on earth. Once the Boss Man had found a replacement, I could hightail it back Up There, and leave Catherine and her mom in safer hands. It would be the best thing all-round...

The Bigshot Burger Bar was a small diner in what looked like a pretty seedy part of town. It was lit up with neon lights, and it looked like the kinda place you'd head directly for if you were hankering after a large dose of salmonella. I followed Catherine in through the door, and had a good look round. The place was full of rickety chairs and tables, and there was a clapped-out jukebox in one corner. There weren't many people in there, just one man sitting on his own, and a group of about six guys, crammed round a table near the window. Behind the counter a rat-faced man with dark, greasy hair was frying eggs on a griddle. I frowned. I didn't like the idea of Catherine working in that seedy dive one little bit.

"You're late, Lucas!" Rat-face snarled as

Catherine hurried over to the counter. "That's a quid off your wages again."

"Sorry, Mr. Burton," Catherine muttered under her breath, pulling off her coat.

"You lousy piece of scum!" I yelled furiously at him. "She's been out at school all day, as well as looking after her mom! Haven't you got any heart?"

"Get over to Table Five and take their order," Burton the Rat snapped, chucking a couple of burgers on to the griddle. I leaned over the counter, and fixed him with an evil stare. He was even grungier looking close up, with a spotty face and black fingernails. "They've been waiting for ten minutes."

"Yes, Mr Burton. Sorry, Mr Burton." Catherine jammed the stupid frilly cap down on her head, and picked up a pencil and pad. She looked tired out. My blood boiled.

"Say, Mr Rat-face Burton," I hissed. "I can tell you right now that you're definitely not going Up There, know what I mean? You're headed in a different direction altogether, you greasy little no-brain."

"Hey! Are we ever going to get any service over here?"

A blond guy, who was one of the group by the jukebox, was standing on his chair, yelling at the top of his voice while his friends roared with laughter. "We could be dead of malnutrition in the next five minutes!"

Burger Burton glared at Catherine.

"Get on with it, Lucas."

"Yes, Mr Burton." Catherine scuttled off across the room.

"Moron," I muttered furiously before I followed her.

"Hi." Catherine gave the group of guys a weary smile, and flicked open her order pad. I stood close beside her, glaring at them, daring them to treat her badly. "What would you like?"

"Not much from you, sweetheart, that's for sure," said the blond guy with a leer. "Hey, are those all your own spots, or are you looking after them for a few hundred friends?"

The other guys at the table fell about laughing. I clenched my fists, wishing I could thump them. Hard.

"Shut up, you boneheads!" I yelled. OK, they couldn't see or hear me, but there wasn't anything else I could do just now.

"Do you want to order?" Catherine asked quietly. I glanced across at her. Her face was blank, closed in, as if somebody had wiped away all the expression, like an eraser on a chalkboard.

"Yeah. Three coffees, two cokes, a strawberry milkshake and burger and chips all round," snapped Blond Creepo. "And make it fast, Zit-Face."

Catherine wrote the order on her pad without speaking and walked off. I stayed behind. I was dying to tell BC exactly what I thought of him, somehow.

"What a dog, eh?" said BC to the other guys, grinning from ear to ear. "Don't reckon she should be working around food, do you? She's a health hazard!"

"Yeah, it's enough to put you off your grub, innit?" said one of the gang, who was a dead ringer for Bugs Bunny.

"You're a bunch of brain-dead dorks," I said loudly and clearly. Catherine was coming back towards us now, carrying a tray piled with drinks. "Don't talk to her like that again," I advised them through gritted teeth. "Or you'll be sorry."

"Hey, Spotty," crowed BC, as Catherine placed a cup of coffee in front of him. "Why don't you try washing your hair with shampoo instead of chip fat?" His friends collapsed into gurgles of laughter, and I nearly burst a blood vessel. Catherine simply put the other glasses down on the table and walked away without a word.

"OK, wiseguy!" I snapped. "You've had your fun, and right here's where you start paying!"

I leaned across the table, and flipped the steaming cup of coffee right over. The boiling liquid shot forward in a stream, connecting with Blond Creepo's crotch in about one second flat. His reaction was indisputably satisfactory.

"Yeaah!" he shrieked, leaping to his feet. "I've burnt me privates!"

"Enjoy," I told him as I turned away, smirking to myself. Hey, maybe this Guardian-Angel-type-thing had its good points after all! If it just meant dealing with brain-dead morons like BC and his gang, I could handle that. No sweat. It was the thought of trying to deal with all of Catherine's other problems that cracked me up.

My next job as a (temporary) Guardian Angel was to check that Catherine was OK. I glanced round the café, but she seemed to have disappeared. That girl sure had the hide of an elephant, I thought to myself as I went over to the counter. She didn't seem to care that she had no friends at school, and she'd kept her temper right under control when those creeps had been needling her.

"Hey, Lucas!" Bigshot Burton had kicked open a door behind the counter, and was screeching at the top of his voice. "Hurry up with that pack of burgers!"

I slipped behind the counter, avoiding Burton like the plague, and through the door. There was some kind of storeroom behind there, and it stank real bad. There were sacks of potatoes lying around, and a couple of filthy-looking freezers down at the other end. Catherine was standing there, holding a pack of frozen burgers in one hand. She was crying without making a sound, shoulders heaving, tears streaming down her face.

I guess it was right at that moment when I realized that I'd become what you'd call "emotionally involved". But if there's one thing I hate, it's seeing someone cry. Not just girls, anyone. Kids, babies, my mom when our old cat died, my dad when his brother had lung cancer. It just cracks me up.

Slowly I leaned forward and put my arm tentatively round Catherine's shoulders. She didn't even know I was there, and she didn't stop crying. But to me, it meant something important. It meant that I was in this thing now. No going back.

But first of all I had a few details to sort out

with Jo-Jo. Because if I was going to see this thing through, I was going to do it Sinatra-style. My way.

CHAPTER FOUR

"I don't get it, man. I just don't get it." Jo-Jo was pacing up and down, looking about as agitated as it's possible for an old hippy to get. "I mean, like one minute you want out, the next minute you want back in. What's going down here?"

"I just changed my mind, that's all." I was temporarily back Up There after I'd escorted Catherine home from the burger bar, and watched her stay up till past midnight, finishing her homework. I was even more determined than ever to give the poor chick a helping hand. And in true Aidan Douglas style, I'd come up with a mind-blowing idea. But I knew I had to take things kinda slowly. Still, the Boss Man was pretty hot on forgiveness and second chances and all that jazz.

"Jo-Jo?" I asked nervously. "The Boss isn't mad at me, is he?"

"He ain't happy." Jo-Jo shot me a glare that would've killed me at twenty paces if I hadn't been dead already. "Catherine Lucas is, like, a top priority case. We ain't got time to pussyfoot around, dig?"

"I dig – I mean, I understand," I agreed eagerly. This was it. My big chance. "That's why I've come up with an outta-this-world, mega-hot brainwave."

"And I ask myself, man, do I really want to hear this?" Jo-Jo muttered mournfully, burying his head in his hands.

"Aw, come on, Jo-Jo, have faith. This is foolproof!"

"It'd need to be." Jo-Jo looked at me suspiciously. "Come on then, brother. Lay it on me."

"OK, get this," I gabbled really fast, so that I could explain everything properly before he freaked. "I go back to earth properly this time – like, visibly, and…"

Too late. Jo-Jo freaked.

"Are you mad?" You've got to be out of your tiny, microscopic little mind!"

I had already anticipated Jo-Jo's reaction, and I was ready for him.

"Give me one good reason why not."

"OK. Here's one." Jo-Jo threw me an icy glare. "Basically, kid, you're dead. And we can't have dead people walking around down below all over the place."

"Just let me explain…"

"You know how many times a GA's gone back down there like *visibly* in the last thirty thousand years or so? I'll tell you - only five times! It's like the very, very, very, very, VERY last resort for a Guardian Angel, man –"

"OK, OK, I hear what you're saying," I interrupted soothingly. "But –"

"No buts, man. No ifs. No chance. No way." Jo-Jo paced up and down the cloud. "The Boss Man wouldn't wear it for a second."

"Maybe if you kissed up to him just a bit?" I suggested tentatively.

"Kissed up to him?" Jo-Jo squeaked, outraged. "This is, like, the Supreme Being we're talking about here!"

"Just give me five minutes to explain the whole thing, Jo-Jo. Five minutes," I argued desperately. "That's all I need to make you see what a pretty damn brilliant idea this is."

Jo-Jo sighed.

"Go ahead then, dude. And this'd better be good."

"OK. Picture the scene." I leapt eagerly on to a nearby cloud. "A poor, downtrodden babe – no friends, no money, no life."

"Guess you must mean Catherine Lucas,"

Jo-Jo said with a grin.

"Got it in one," I snapped back smartly. I had to make this work. My future visits to earth depended on it. "A new guy turns up at the school; good-looking, charming, smart and driving all the girls wild."

"Whoever can that be, man?"

"Me, Jo-Jo, me. Look, haven't you sussed yet?" I stared at him impatiently. "Everybody's amazed when stunning guy falls for gross chick, takes her out on a date, spends time with her and transforms her whole life. Result: Lucas feels better about herself, becomes more confident, makes new friends and everything ends happily." I grinned proudly. "What do you think?"

My heart sank. Jo-Jo was shaking his head gloomily.

"I don't think so, man."

"Why not?" I said urgently. "It's brilliant. It's foolproof. It can't fail."

"The Boss Man won't like it," Jo-Jo said firmly. "He don't approve of GAs and LPs getting, like, too close. Things can turn heavy."

"Aw, come on, Jo-Jo," I scoffed. "This is Catherine Lucas we're talking about here. I'll only be faking the hots for her. NO WAY am I really gonna get involved. After all," smugly I played my trump card, "you admitted yourself that I was a big hit with the babes."

"I only meant that with your, like, experience of chicks you'd have a pretty good idea which way to handle Catherine," Jo-Jo said grumpily. "I sure didn't mean you could mosey on back down to Earth as if you weren't dead, and chat her up."

"Jo-Jo..."

"Remember what I told you about how a GA's supposed to operate? Remember subtle? Remember in-the-background?"

"Jo-Jo, I..."

"It's a big risk, man. This is somebody's real life you're goin' to be messing around with."

"JO-JO! It's our only chance!" I danced about in frustrated impatience on my cloud. "Look, you've seen how babes fall over themselves to get a date with me!"

"Watch it, man. You'll need a new size halo if your head, like, expands any further."

"And Catherine's going to feel pretty good about herself if she's the girl I hit on out of all the babes in the school." I stared desperately at Jo-Jo, willing him to agree. "It could be the kickstart she needs to get her life back on track."

Jo-Jo didn't say anything for a few minutes.

I waited silently too, to give his hippy brain time to come round to the idea.

"Well, yeah, it sounds, like, pretty foolproof, man," he admitted grudgingly at last. "But, hey, I still don't know how the Boss will take it."

I played my final ace.

"You got any better ideas?"

Silence. I held my breath.

"Negative," Jo-Jo said at last. "OK, I'll see what I can do. But don't, like, get your hopes up. The Boss Man might blow a fuse." He gathered up his robes, and floated away, calling back over his shoulder: "Hang loose while I check it out. And if you see any thunderbolts coming your way, man – duck."

All I had to do now was wait. I sat down on a cloud and watched a couple of kids playing frisbee with their haloes, feeling pretty damn pleased with myself. I mean, OK, I really was worried about Catherine (just call me a born loser) Lucas, and I did want to help her. But I sure intended to do yours truly, Aidan Douglas, a bit of good too, in the process. I was going to make sure that I had plenty of opportunities to enjoy myself back on earth, in between sorting out The Lucas. I mean, I was always pretty smart at that looking-after-numero-uno type thing.

Jo-Jo was on his way back. You could spot

that gross purple headband a mile away. I leapt to my feet.

"Well?" I looked at him hopefully. "I didn't see any thunderbolts."

"You're in, man."

"I'm in? What, you mean he said yes?" My mouth fell open.

"Believe it, man. And I had to lay some pretty heavy vibes on him to get him to agree." Jo-Jo produced a sheaf of papers from under his arm, and tried to look business-like. "Right, let's talk rules and regulations."

I wasn't listening. I was too busy performing my legendary back-flip with double somersault, the one that had always driven the girls wild after the basketball team had won a home game.

"Hey, all right! Let's get this show on the road!"

"Hold it right there!" Jo-Jo snapped furiously. "This is real heavy stuff here, Aidan. It ain't some kind of game, you know."

"No. No. Sure." I forced myself to look solemn, while I was chillin' out inside. I was going back to earth. Not invisible this time. Real. With hands that could touch things, arms that could hold things, lips which could kiss – well, whatever I wanted to kiss. I could hardly handle the excitement. "Anything I need to know before I go?"

"Plenty." Jo-Jo fixed me with a hard stare. "And make sure you listen good this time, huh? You turn up at Catherine's school. They're expecting you - it's all been fixed up."

"Fine," I said happily. I couldn't wait to check out those gorgeous British babes. In person this time.

"And no foolin' around."

"Foolin' around?" I put on my wide-eyed, innocent look, which had always got the girls drooling back on earth. "Wouldn't dream of it."

"Just remember you're not a real Live Person, and it'll be cool," Jo-Jo said warningly. "Any foolin' around, and you'll be hauled back up here faster than you can say angel cake."

Foolin' around seemed to cover everything I'd enjoyed when I was alive. My face fell.

"Anything else?" I asked sourly.

"Yeah. About you and Catherine. Like, absolutely NO physical contact, except in the line of duty."

"Look, I already told you," I broke in impatiently. "Nothing heavy's going to happen. Lucas is bound to fall pretty hard for me, but I can handle it." I grinned. "I'll be gentle with her, don't worry."

"Glad to hear it, dude, because once you're

down there in person, you're kinda on your own. I won't be able to be in contact with you so much. So you got to report back to me Up Here every night."

"What, you mean you won't be nagging, I mean, talking in my ear the whole time?" I said eagerly.

"That's the deal." Jo-Jo looked at me suspiciously. "Think you can handle it?"

"I guess I'll just have to struggle along on my own," I sighed, smothering an ecstatic grin. At last, a chance to PAAAAAAARTY!

"Last thing." Jo-Jo consulted his notes. "This is the difficult bit, man. No contact with your family in the States. No calls. No letters. Nothing."

I didn't say anything for a moment. Then I nodded slowly.

"OK." Secretly I wasn't sure I could keep to that. I'd just have to wait and see.

"Groovy." Jo-Jo slapped me heartily on the back and nearly bust my spine. "You ready then, man?"

"As ready as I'll ever be. Apart from…" I glanced down at myself. "Hey, Jo-Jo, I'm gonna get fitted out in some decent clothes, aren't I? I mean, I'm gonna start a riot if I walk into that school looking like this."

"Yeah, the halo's a dead giveaway. Relax, man." I could hardly see Jo-Jo now as a bright light swirled around me, starting at my feet and moving upwards. His voice was growing fainter too. "It'll all be sorted. Trust me."

The light grew brighter and brighter till I had to close my eyes against the flash. There was a deafening noise like the sound of the wind rushing past me, and then that died away. I could hear cars and people and birds singing. I opened my eyes. I was back on earth again, standing outside those ol' school gates.

"Wow!" I muttered, blinking hard. "Far out!"

I glanced down at myself again, and freaked somewhat seriously. My angel outfit had vanished. I was now wearing a green and silver kaftan, open-toed sandals, a green headband and a string of lovebeads. I nearly threw up on the spot.

"Jo-Jo!" I hissed furiously.

"Just my little joke, man," said a faint but distinctly smug voice in my ear. "Try these for size. Oh, and good luck."

There was another quick, blinding flash of light, and the revolting kaftan vanished. What replaced it was better, but only just. A grey-flannel-type-thing jacket, black pants, white shirt and, get this, a *tie*. I'd heard that kids in England had to wear school uniform, but this was double gross. A few minor stylistic adjustments were definitely called for. Quickly I rolled up the sleeves of the jacket, loosened off the tie, undid my collar button. Just a touch less gross. Still, at least my feet looked OK. I walked backwards a few paces, admiring my black and white Reeboks, and collided with a woman rushing past carrying a pile of shopping.

"Why don't you look where you're going, young man?" she snapped, manouevring her way around me as I stood with my mouth open.

She could see me. I was really, really *real*. I was back on earth, and I was real. Emotion swelled up inside me. If Mom, Dad, Buster and Susan were here right now, they'd be able to see me too. They'd be pretty shocked, sure, but they'd be able to see me. They'd be able to touch me. And they were only an ocean away.

There was a telephone booth on the corner of the street. Without thinking, I ran headlong towards it. I guess you guys think that Americans are always telling their family how much they love them, right? I mean, that's how it is in the movies. But I couldn't remember ever saying "I love you" to my mom or dad, not since I was about six anyway. But I wanted to say it now. I wanted to say it so much, I felt as if I was exploding with love inside.

I squashed into the kiosk, and feverishly checked the instructions on phoning abroad. I'd have to speak to the operator, tell her I wanted to telephone the States collect or reversed charges or whatever they called it over here. Breathlessly I picked up the receiver.

"Put the phone down, man." Jo-Jo's voice at the other end of the line almost made me leap out of my skin. "You won't get through. Just put the phone down."

Slowly I let the receiver drop back on to its cradle. I leaned my forehead against the cool glass, and fought down a massive lump in my throat. Hey, you birdbrain, I yelled silently at myself, that was a dumb idea. What would I have done when Mom picked up the phone? Said "Hi, Mom. Aidan calling"? She'd probably have hit the floor at the speed of light. And it would be pretty hard to convince them that it really was me on the other end of the line. My parents would probably think it was a hoax and get really upset. Stupid idea, Aidan.

It took ten minutes of deep-breathing and straight-talking to calm myself down. Then I went out of the phone booth, and back up the street. The schoolyard was deserted. I guess I must've missed the buzzer for morning class. Feeling ultra-nervous, I tiptoed carefully up to the entrance doors, and walked smash into the glass, almost bending my nose into a permanently different shape.

"Ouch!" Gotta remember I wasn't invisible any more, I told myself grimly, rubbing my throbbing face. Walking through glass doors was a definite no-no. Picture the scene. I'm rushed off to hospital, and the doctors discover the first teenager in the world with no pulse. Yep, this coming-back-to-life-and-reality-type-thing sure meant a lot of stuff to remember.

Still, it had its good points. Like now. Two blonde babes were walking down the school corridor in my direction and staring hard at me. They looked pretty cool, even in those sick-making black skirts and grey sweaters and stripy ties (jeez, the English sure have got a thing about ties). As we drew level, I ran my hand through my hair and winked at them. Aidan Douglas Chat-Up Technique Number 12. Never fails.

"Hiya, girls."

Cue hysterical giggles, and much digging of elbows into each other's ribs.

"Hi," the one with the big blue eyes managed to get out at last. "You new?"

"Yep." I treated them both to a lazy half-smile. The one I'd practised in front of the mirror for hours. They both practically melted into a pool of quivering Jell-O at my feet. Boy, even though I was dead, I could still cut it. And that was going to make my Masterplan To Save The Lucas a piece of cake. "I'm looking for Mrs Bradley's class."

"Down the corridor, turn right," drooled the other girl. "You American?"

"Got it in one. See you around." I sauntered off down the corridor, knowing without needing to look back over my shoulder that they were watching my every move. Hey, if you're the kind of guy I am, you've just got to get used to this universal-adoration-and-babes-falling-at-your-feet-type-thing. And, with all the other females in the school swarming round me like bees to honey, poor old Catherine Lucas just wasn't going to believe her luck when I turned the full force of the Aidan Douglas Charm Machine on her. Cue instant transformation of her boring, depressing and friendless life, and much rejoicing Up There. There was just the one problem here. Not only did I have to ask Lucas out, I also had to pretend that I actually liked her. Not easy. I was going to have to bite the bullet, and be seen around town with a toad on my arm, instead of the gorgeous babes I'd been used to in the past. Still, I was hoping there'd be a few opportunities at least to "fool around". As Jo-Jo would say.

There was a low babble of noise inside the classroom. That stopped immediately as I opened the door and went in. What seemed like a hundred pairs of eyes looked up from books and newspapers and magazines, swivelled round to the doorway and focused on little ol' me. For a moment I froze. I'd remembered to leave my halo behind, hadn't I? 'Course I had. I'd just forgotten what it was like to be the new boy in class.

"Aidan Douglas?" The concrete-headed crone I'd seen on my first visit was sitting at a desk at the front of the class, looking at me enquiringly.

"Yeah. I mean – yes." I advanced into the room, throwing a quick, cautious look round. As far as I could see, Lucas wasn't there. As far as I was concerned, I couldn't give a damn. There was plenty of gorgeous scenery – blonde, brunette and redhead – to look at.

"Welcome to Class 4A. I'm your form tutor, Mrs Bradley." The crone, aka Mrs Bradley, stood up and looked me over as if I was a dead mouse. "I understand you've just come over from the USA. I do hope you won't have too many problems settling in."

She made it sound like I'd just dropped in from Mars. I gave her my just-for-teachers, star-pupil, confiding smile.

"I guess I'll just have to do my best."

Mrs B. turned a shade pink. Wow. If I could get to her, Lucas was going to be what is commonly known as a surefire thing.

"Well, don't hesitate to ask if there's anything you don't understand. Now I'll sort you out a timetable, and someone will show you the cloakrooms. Daniel, if you wouldn't mind..."

"OK, Miss." Daniel Whoever-he-was stood up. He looked OK, kinda dark-haired and ordinary, but I'd rather have had the blonde babe to his left who kept simpering at me. Still, mustn't get impatient. Lucas had to come first, or Jo-Jo would get his hippy headband in a twist.

"You're over from the States then?" Daniel asked me as we left the room.

"Yeah, we've moved to England for a year," I said, improvising wildly. "My Dad's got a job over here. So what's this seat of hallowed learning like then?"

Daniel grinned at me.

"Pretty different from your school back home, I suppose."

"Oh, I don't know about that. I guess schools are pretty much the same the world over." I winked. "Hey, you can explain something to me though."

"What?"

"Why you Brits have got a thing about ties." I grinned and flipped mine up into the air. "I feel like a bank teller in this get-up."

Just then a pretty blonde walked past us, givin' me that ol' sideways glance. Quick as a flash I flipped her a cheeky wink, turning round to get a better eyeful as she went down the corridor, blushing all over her face.

"Hey, Daniel," I hissed urgently at him. "D'you know which class that blonde's in?"

I never got an answer to my question. At precisely that moment, I was knocked sideways as a mad bull charged round the corner of the corridor, smashed straight into me and mowed me ruthlessly down. A stinging pain shot through my knee and my elbow, and I staggered, clutching at the wall for support.

"Why the hell can't you look where you're going!" spat a very familiar voice. Wheezing, I looked up into Catherine Lucas's angry face.

Correction. Very angry face.

"Why can't I look where I'm going!" I repeated, righteous anger boiling up inside me. This babe had a nerve. "*You* were the one who came round that corner like a Sherman tank!"

"I haven't got time to stand here arguing." Lucas brushed past me, and I backed hastily away from her. She had a glint in her eye that made me somewhat nervous. "Just stay out of my way from now on, you brain-dead moron!" she flung at me menacingly before she stomped off down the corridor.

"Don't worry, I will!" I yelled furiously after her. Too late, I remembered. This was the girl I was supposed to be giving all my tender loving care to. Whoops.

"Don't let Catherine get to you," Daniel said to me soothingly. "Nothing personal. She's like that with everybody. I reckon she's got some major problems at home, but nobody knows what."

"Is that right?" Gingerly I massaged my aching elbow. The Aidan Douglas Masterplan had just gotten off to a seriously unpromising start.

CHAPTER FIVE

"Well, well, well." Jo-Jo looked at me, consulted his clipboard and shook his head. "Not good, man. Not good. In, like, plain English, a disaster."

"It wasn't that bad," I argued bitterly, rubbing the technicolour bruise on my arm. "We just didn't hit it off straightaway, that's all."

"You mean, like, she hates the sight of you."

"No way." I hoped I sounded more confident than I felt. Which was zilch. "Look, she's just got a downer on me because I bumped into her, that's all. She'll get over it."

Jo-Jo scratched his head thoughtfully.

"You sure about that? She seems like one strong-minded chick."

"I haven't met a girl yet that I couldn't sweet-talk my way round," I said modestly. "So why should Catherine Lucas be any different?" But I couldn't help secretly feeling just a bit uneasy deep down inside. I'd die before I let on to Jo-Jo though. In a manner of speaking. "Anyway, I've already started my campaign. I went and apologized to her later and she was pretty OK about it."

"Yeah?" Jo-Jo fixed me with a beady eye, and then looked down at his clipboard again. "According to, like, information received, her actual words were: "Push off, you slimy creep, and look where you're going in future.""

"Yeah. Well. Something like that." I blushed, and shuffled my feet. A slimy creep? Anything less slimy or creep-like than my well-appointed self would be hard to imagine. "Words to that effect."

"And when you tried to shoot her a line after school…" There was a hint of an annoying smirk on Jo-Jo's face, as he read aloud from the clipboard.

"AIDAN: Can I carry your books home for you?

"CATHERINE: Not you again! What do you think this is, *Little House on the Prairie*? Get lost!"

I blushed a deeper red.

"If you know all this already, why do I have to trail up here every night to make a report?" I demanded sourly. "I mean, you lot are all-seeing and all-knowing, aren't you?"

"Sure. But we want to hear your side of the story too." Jo-Jo grinned at me. "Trouble is, you seem to be tellin' a story that's a whole lot different."

"OK, OK," I cut in impatiently, "I know my first day on the job was pretty lousy, but it'll be better tomorrow. I swear it will." I mean, once Catherine realized that she did like me after all, things would be a whole lot easier. But, jeez, was I having to work hard to get her to realize it.

"We'll see how things go then, man." Jo-Jo tucked the clipboard away under his arm. "Let's hope the fatal Douglas charm gets to work soon, or we're history."

"It will," I promised him grimly. OK. I'd been holding back up till now. But from tomorrow it was going to be no-holds-barred.

"Can't you take a hint, you moron?"

It was the following morning. I was in the schoolyard before class, and Catherine Lucas was glaring at me with murder in her eyes. "You're really starting to get on my nerves."

"Hey, all I said was hi, how's it going and you're lookin' cool today!" I protested, aggrieved. I'd seen her come through the gate, on time for once, and immediately I'd zoomed over there to begin my Kissing-Up Campaign. "What's your problem?"

"You are." Catherine clutched her forehead as if she was in pain. "Everywhere I turn, you're always there, right behind me. You're making me paranoid!"

"What's your problem, sweetheart?" I smiled at her, and moved in slightly closer for the kill. "Look, I just want to make a few friends, that's all."

Lucas backed away from me as smartly as if I had chronic bad breath.

"I prefer to choose my own friends, thanks," she snapped tartly.

"Yeah? Well, you sure seem a bit light in that department." The words were out before I could stop them. "And it doesn't take a genius to see why."

There was a tense silence between us that lasted uncomfortably long. For about fifteen seconds Catherine and I were staring into each other's eyes like boxers squaring up before a big fight. I'd never noticed before, but once you looked past her skin problems, her eyes were arresting. Deep-sea blue with shades of green. She didn't say a word and neither did I. Then she spun round and walked off.

Well done, Aidan, I thought in silent

mortification, you big-mouthed, insensitive ape.

"Hi, mate." Somebody came up behind me and slapped me on the back. It was that kid Daniel Greene. "Hey, you a glutton for punishment or what? Wasn't that Catherine Lucas I just saw you talking to?"

"Yep," I said gloomily. "She hates me."

"Don't worry about it. She hates everybody." Daniel shrugged. "Why're you so interested in her anyway?"

"I'm not," I said quickly. "I just feel sorry for her, I guess."

"You don't need to bother about Catherine Lucas. Half the girls in our class are madly in love with you already." Daniel winked at me. "They're all dying to know who you're going to take to the school disco on Friday night."

"Yeah?" I said absently. That look in Catherine's eyes was still buggin' me. But after a few seconds what Daniel had said finally filtered through. "A school dance, huh? Friday, you said?"

"Yep. You going to ask one of the girls?"

"Definitely." My self-confidence, which had taken a bit of a battering lately, rose a notch or two. Surely not even Catherine Lucas would be able to resist an invite to mosey on into the dance on the arm of the best-lookin' boy in the school. This could be the answer to all my problems. And hers. "How about you, Dan my man? You got a girl yourself?"

"Er, not at the moment." Daniel turned pink. He was obviously the shy type, but, hey, some girls go for that. And with a few lessons from The Master, he could go far.

"Then good ol' Aidan's here to give you a helping hand, my friend." I grinned at him jauntily, feeling pretty much my old self again. All I had to do was to get Catherine to agree to come to the dance with me. Picture the scene. A moonlit night, an embrace, a kiss under the stars, and I'd be well on the way to sorting out her life. No sweat.

For a spaced-out old hippy, Jo-Jo had fixed things up pretty good. He'd made sure that all the classes I had timetabled were the same as Catherine's, so that wherever she went, I was always in the same group. No wonder the poor babe was getting paranoid. Still, I didn't have much time for hustling her while we were studying. I was too busy trying to cope with algebra and the French Revolution and Shakespeare, after three months' vacation being dead. (I made a mental note to try and check things out with old Will, once I got back up there. If I could find him. Jo-Jo had been looking for the last twenty years, and he still hadn't managed to find Jimi Hendrix.) Once or twice that morning in between math and essays and maps of the world, I'd glanced across the room at Catherine, but she was never looking in my direction.

So it wasn't until lunchtime that I finally got my chance. Dan and I were in the hot, noisy canteen, queuing up for food, when I spotted Catherine sitting by herself at a corner of one of the long tables. I grinned to myself. Countdown to victory.

"Yes, love?" said the lady at the serving-hatch enquiringly.

"Fries, please – sorry, chips. Salad. And some of that pie, thanks."

"Sure you don't want a burger instead?" She smiled at me. "I thought you Americans loved them."

"We do. That's why I don't want one, thanks." I'd had a burger yesterday. Big mistake. It had tasted like dogmeat.

"Where do you want to sit?" Daniel asked me as I collected a glass of water and an apple.

"Follow me," I said airily. Carrying my tray high like a trophy, I strode confidently across the canteen in Catherine's direction, scattering juniors before me like flies. Watch and learn,

Dan. Watch and learn.

"Mind if we join you?" I put my tray down on the table and gave Catherine a winsome smile.

"It's a free country," she said shortly.

Wow. She hadn't actually said yes, but then she hadn't actually said no either. One small step for mankind maybe, but a giant step for Aidan Douglas. Eagerly I slid into the seat next to her, ignoring the bewildered look on Daniel's face as he sat down opposite. I was almost home already. Jeez, why had I ever even considered the possibility of failure? I could just imagine Jo-Jo's incredulous face if he was watching me right now. Seeing me effortlessly breezing in and putting Catherine's world to rights.

"Hey, Catherine." I leaned back, and draped one arm casually across the back of her chair. "How're you then?"

"I'm fine." Catherine swung round so that she could look at me. And – sit down for this one if you aren't already – she was actually smiling at me. Only a kind of half-smile. Well, maybe a quarter of a smile, just at the corners of her mouth. But she *was* smiling. Mind blowing. She had nice, white even teeth, which I'd never noticed before. "But I'd feel even better if you stopped following me around all the time."

I gave her my special, lazy grin, and turned on the charm.

"Hey, if you're gonna smile at me like that, what choice have I got?"

"Oh, I'm not smiling at you, you slimy creep." Catherine reached across the table. "I'm smiling because I know what's going to happen next." Then she neatly flipped over my glass of water, and a stream of ice-cold liquid poured out all over my thighs.

"Hey!" Furiously I leapt to my feet. Seriously wrong move. Rivers of water flowed down the legs of my pants, and all the kids sitting near us started to snigger. "You crazy idiot! What did you do that for?"

Without answering, Catherine picked up her empty plate and walked off, leaving me wet and fuming. Jeez, I sure wasn't used to letting a female have the last word.

"Aidan?" Daniel was looking at me across the table, shaking his head. "You know those tips you were going to give me about how to chat up girls? I reckon I'll pass, thanks."

"Shut up, willya, and get me a napkin or something," I snapped. What did I have to do to convince this girl to take me seriously, I asked myself in silent despair. She acted like she didn't find me attractive at all. I mean, it just wasn't natural. Never, in the whole of my (short) life had I ever come across a girl like Catherine Lucas.

Daniel seemed pretty impressed too, the moron. He couldn't stop talking about Catherine's vicious and totally unprovoked attack on me all afternoon.

"She's got some nerve, I'll give her that," he said for maybe the ten thousandth time as we messed about with test-tubes and sulphuric acid. We were in Mr Baxter's chemistry class, the last one of the day. "Looks like there's at least one girl in school you can't sweet-talk your way round, mate."

"I guess I should be glad there wasn't sulphuric acid in that glass," I muttered darkly, pouring some into a test-tube. "I can't believe she did that to me, not after..."

"After what?"

"Nothing." I'd been going to say after I'd leapt to her rescue at the Bigshot Burger Bar, and dished out exactly the same treatment to Blond Creepo. I cast an injured look across the room to where Catherine was working on her own, head bent over her project.

"What *is* it between you two anyway?" Daniel looked at me curiously. "You don't really fancy her, do you?"

Luckily Baxter announced that it was only five minutes to the home bell and it was time to clean up, so I avoided the question. I glanced across the room again, and saw that Catherine was standing by the sink, rinsing test-tubes.

"I'll wash our tubes, OK?"

"OK." Daniel raised an eyebrow at me. "But I reckon you're wasting your time."

I was beginning to wonder if he was right, but I couldn't give up now. If I couldn't get Catherine Lucas to play ball, my time on Earth was running out fast. Determinedly I headed over to the sink, clutching my rack of test-tubes.

"Hi, Aidan." My path was blocked by one of the girls in the class – Emma Freeman, blonde, blue-eyed and beautiful. "You coming to the disco on Friday?"

"Er, yep." I shot an agonized glance over Emma's shoulder. Catherine was still at the sink, but for how long? "'Scuse me, Emma," I pushed my way past her. She didn't look too pleased, but I'd just have to live with it. I hurried on over to the sink.

"Hey, Catherine." I reached out and tapped her lightly on the shoulder. Two things happened. First, the home bell sounded.

Second, Catherine leapt a mile into the air and dropped the rack of test tubes she was holding. They crashed to the floor and smashed to pieces.

"What's going on?" Baxter leapt up from his desk at the front of the room, looking ready to kill the perpetrator of this heinous crime.

"Sorry, sir. I dropped them. My fault." I don't know what made me say it. Maybe it was just because Catherine looked so tired and depressed. Maybe it was because I knew she'd have to pay for them and she couldn't afford to. Or maybe it was because it *was* my fault for startling her. I don't know, so don't ask me why.

"You'll have to stay and clear up that mess, Douglas," boomed Baxter over the noise of thirty students hastily packing up their books. "And there's a charge for broken test-tubes, I'm afraid."

"OK, Sir. Fine." Anything was fine by me at the moment, what with Catherine standing and staring at me as if she couldn't believe her ears and eyes. We didn't speak a word to each other as kids and teacher cleared out of the lab at speed. In about thirty seconds flat we were the only two people left in the room.

"I'll see you outside, Aidan, OK?" Daniel

called from the doorway.

"OK." I didn't take my eyes from Catherine's face.

"Why did you do that?" she said at last as Daniel went off down the corridor.

"Well, it was my fault." I fumbled for the right words, feeling – now this is weird – a bit *shy*. Aidan Douglas, shy. A world first. "I startled you. Sorry."

There was silence for a moment or two.

"I think that's the first honest thing you've said to me in the past two days," Catherine said quietly.

"It – it is?" My eyes widened. She was probably right. She *was* right.

"I'll help you clear it up." Catherine smiled at me. Not a quarter smile or a half-smile. But a real smile this time. And you know what? She looked almost OK when she smiled.

"Thanks." A secret warmth welled up inside me. I'd done it. I'd won Catherine over, and all it had taken was a bit of real sincerity. I was suddenly on a high. Go for it, Aidan. "Hey, listen, how would you like to come to the school dance on Friday night with me?"

Catherine had gone over to a cupboard by the teacher's desk. She turned round slowly, a broom in her hand.

"What did you say?"

"I just asked you for a date…" My confident smile died away as I saw that familiar cold, blank look fill her eyes again.

"Oh, I get it." Catherine walked over to me, still clutching the broom. I glanced at it nervously. "This is some stupid bet, isn't it? And that's what you've got to do to win: go out with the ugliest girl in the class."

"What bet?" I asked, bewildered. Catherine didn't answer. She just shoved the broom into my hand with a force that nearly broke my wrist. Two seconds later she was gone.

Good one, Aidan, my man. You just blew it. Spectacularly.

CHAPTER SIX

I'd given Jo-Jo strict instructions about the kind of clothes I wanted to wear for the school disco, and he'd come across with the whole deal. Well-worn jeans, plain white T-shirt, black leather jacket and baseball cap. Kinda James Deanish. I looked down at myself with serious satisfaction as I stood on the doorstep outside Catherine's house. I looked cooler than cool. I looked so cool, I was hot. Any girl who got an eyeful of me at the dance tonight did so at entirely her own risk.

Yeah, you heard me right. I was standing outside Catherine Lucas's house. And no, she hadn't suddenly realized what an all-out great guy I was, and agreed to go to the dance with me after all. In fact, we'd spent the last three days playing a real cat-and-mouse game. I'd spent all my time hangin' around trying to get her into conversation, and win her over with my somewhat irresistible charm, and she'd spent all her time blanking me out. And boy, was Catherine Lucas hot at blanking me out. She could have ignored for her country, she was so damn good at it. And get this, I was even beginning to feel a grudging respect for her. Hey, no babe had ever stood out against *my* charm for so long. In the last three days, I'd got precisely nowhere. As Jo-Jo never stopped reminding me.

But, true to form, the brilliant brain of Aidan Douglas had risen to the occasion with yet another foolproof plan. Humming "Heaven Must be Missing an Angel" softly to myself, I rang the Lucas doorbell.

I had to wait quite a while for anyone to come. Meanwhile, I said my prayers and hoped the Boss Man wasn't too busy to hear. They were answered when the door swung open and there sat Catherine's mom in her wheelchair.

"Yes?" She looked at me in astonishment. I guessed they didn't get many visitors.

"Hi. I'm Aidan Douglas, a friend of Catherine's from school," I said breezily. "I thought I'd call in on my way to the school disco. See if Catherine wanted to come with me."

Mrs Lucas's tired, lined face lit up like a Christmas tree. She was kinda pretty, I guess. She looked a lot like Catherine.

"Oh, I'm sure she would, dear. Come in. She's in the bath at the moment. I hope you don't mind waiting."

"No problem." Round one to me. Cheering myself inwardly, I stepped into the hallway. I was relying somewhat heavily on the fact that Catherine wouldn't want to beat me to a verbal pulp in front of her mom. OK, pretty lousy trick, I know. But I sure couldn't think of anything else to do. And it looked like Mom had already come down firmly on my side.

"Come in, Aidan." Mrs Lucas led me into the ultra-depressing lounge I'd seen on my first visit. "Have a seat. Cathy should be down in a minute." She looked at me eagerly. "Have you two been friends long?"

"Not long." I sat down gingerly on one of the lumpy armchairs. It felt like all the springs had been taken out and replaced by rocks. "I only started school this week. Catherine's been helping me to settle in." Well, I could hardly say that we'd been at each other's throats for the last week, could I?

"I'm glad." Mrs. Lucas smiled at me wearily. "I worry about her, you know. She has such a lot to do, looking after me and coping with school..."

"Don't worry," I broke in, feeling like a

complete rat. "I'll make sure she has a great time tonight."

At that moment the door opened and Catherine came in. She was wearing a bathrobe, and had a towel wrapped round her head. She'd taken two steps into the room when she saw me and stopped dead in her tracks. I leapt hastily to my feet. I'd done two months of a karate course in Junior High. The look on Catherine's face told me I might need it.

"What the hell are you doing here?" she hissed at me in a low, furious voice.

"Aidan's come round to ask if you'd like to go to the school disco with him." Catherine's mom got in first. "Isn't that nice of him?"

I stared innocently across the room at Catherine. Boy, you could almost see her blood pressure rising by the second.

"Yes. Very nice," she ground out through gritted teeth, fixing me with a look of pure, unadulterated hatred. "But I can't go, thanks all the same."

"Hey, why not?" I tipped my baseball cap back on to my head, and grinned challengingly at her. I was sure enjoying getting the upper hand for once. Jeez, she'd outwitted me every step of the way so far. "We'll have a great time."

"I can't leave my mum on her own,"

Catherine said tightly. I mentioned before that she had really expressive eyes. And right now they were expressing "Get out of here, you moron, before I break your neck."

"Of course you can," Mrs Lucas said with grim determination. I certainly didn't need to argue my own case, not with Mom on my side. "You're going out to enjoy yourself just this once, even if Aidan and I have to drag you out kicking and screaming. Now go and get changed."

"But, Mum –"

"I mean it, Catherine. Go and get ready."

Without another word Catherine went out of the room, looking like she'd just swallowed a lemon. Whole. I smiled triumphantly to myself.

"Way to go, Mrs Lucas," I said admiringly.

I was surprised when she winked at me.

"My daughter's very strong-minded, Aidan. But she doesn't always remember where she gets it from! Now, would you like a cup of tea while you're waiting? We haven't got any coffee, I'm afraid."

"Tea's fine." I was beginning to like Mrs Lucas more and more. Hey, anyone who could make Catherine do something she obviously didn't want to was OK by me. By the time the tea was ready, we were chatting away like old buddies, and I was telling her about Mom, Dad, Buster, Susan and home, and how much I missed them.

"So your family aren't over here then." Mrs Lucas looked at me sympathetically. "Who are you living with?"

"My uncle," I improvized quickly. I sure hoped none of the people I'd talked to ever got together and compared notes. I couldn't remember what I'd told who. Or whom. Luckily I didn't need to shoot Mrs L. any more lines because at that moment Catherine came back into the room, and I felt my heart miss a beat.

I guess you've probably heard the story about the Ugly Duckling who turned into a swan. Or the one about the plain girl who takes off her glasses and lets down her hair, and turns into a stunning movie-star type. Well, forget it. Catherine wasn't stunning by a long way. But she'd improved. Her hair was loose around her face, and for once it had that shiny, just-washed look (excuse the ad-speak). She even had some make-up on. Although she was only wearing jeans and a T-shirt, nothing special, they still suited her better than that gross school uniform. Hey, she was never gonna be a real cool babe or anything, but she wasn't half bad.

At least now she looked human.

Except for that wild, just-wait-till-I-get-you-outside-type-glint in her eyes. I gulped. Should have asked Jo-Jo to fit me out with a full suit of body-armour.

"Have a good time then, you two." Mrs Lucas ushered us quickly to the front door before Catherine had a chance to complain again. "And, Aidan, don't let Catherine leave too early. Make sure you stay until the end."

"Don't worry, Mrs L.," I called back with a jaunty wave as we went down the path. "We will."

Catherine muttered something under her breath as she swung open the garden gate, narrowly missing my shins. I couldn't be sure, but it sounded something like "brain-dead moron". Words to that effect, anyway.

We paced along the sidewalk in silence. I was tensed right up, ready for a verbal attack, but nothing happened. I was also mentally practising my karate chops in case of trouble. With a girl like Catherine Lucas, you just couldn't tell.

By the time we reached the corner, though, I was beginning to relax. Hey, credit where credit is most definitely due. I'd finally achieved the impossible. Catherine (get-off-my-case) Lucas was actually on her way to the school dance with yours truly. I injected a bit more of a swagger into my walk, ran my hand casually through my hair and, OK, yeah, I preened myself just a bit. I hoped Jo-Jo was watching right now. Turning to Catherine, I gave her a triumphant smile.

"We're going to have a great time tonight, Cath. Just you and me, gettin' to know each other –"

I froze. Catherine Lucas was no longer at my side. I spun round. She was walking purposefully away in the opposite direction.

"Hey!" Furiously I charged after her and caught her up. "Where you goin'? The school's thataway!"

"I know." Catherine pinned me with a calm but ferocious stare. "But I'm not going to school."

"Hold it right there!" I zipped in front of her and blocked her path. "You're supposed to be coming to the dance with me –"

"That's what you think." Catherine folded her arms and looked at me as if I was a particularly infectious disease. "But I'm not going."

"I'll go back and tell your mom," I threatened her crossly with all the invention and originality of a six-year-old.

"Fine. You do that." Catherine poked me in the chest with her index finger. It hurt. "And if you do, I'll tell her you only asked me to go with you for a bet. I suppose you and that mate of yours Daniel Greene have set this up?"

"Will you stop going on about this lousy bet?" I howled despairingly. "There *is* no bet, get it? No bet! Nil! Zilch! NO BET!"

An old woman who was just walking past us looked at me nervously, and crossed to the other side of the street.

"OK," Catherine said after a few moments of complete silence. "There's no need to shout. You've made your point."

"What?" My jaw hit my chest. "You mean you believe me?"

"'Course I believe you." Catherine nodded calmly. "I've noticed that the end of your nose twitches when you're telling lies."

"It does?" Gingerly I rubbed the end of the organ in question. I'd have to remember that. "So you'll come to the dance with me?"

"Not until we've cleared a few things up first." Catherine sat down on a nearby wall, looking businesslike. "If it's not for a bet, why *do* you want to go out with me?"

"Well," I opened and closed my mouth a

couple of times, but no sound came out. This babe sure had a way of backing a guy into a tight corner. "Er, um. I like you."

"What, you mean you fancy me?"

"Well. Yeah."

What else could I say? I just hoped my nose wasn't twitching too hard. Casually I put up my hand and touched the end of it. It didn't feel as if it was twitching at all.

"Oh." Catherine slowly looked me up and down as if I was a garage sale reject. "There's just one problem."

"What's that?"

"I don't fancy you."

I didn't say anything for maybe thirty seconds. I mean, you have to give a shocking statement like that time to sink in.

"Aw, come on." I managed a feeble little laugh. "You ain't serious. Are you?"

Catherine just looked at me. She was serious. *This* was serious. Never in my whole life had I ever had to beg a girl for a date. The shame of it.

"You mean you really don't want to go out with me?" I stammered, outraged. "What's wrong with me, huh? I mean, I'm good-looking, smart, funny –"

Catherine was shaking her head slowly.

"No offence, Aidan. But you're not my type."

Not her type! I almost choked.

"I suppose we could just be mates though," Catherine went on grudgingly, in the kind of tone she might have used if Count Dracula had asked her to be best friends. "As long as you realize that romance is out."

"Sure. Fine," I said in a small voice. "Whatever you say." It wasn't damn well fine at all really. I didn't *want* to be friends with her. I wanted to be her date. But what else could I do? I could hardly force the girl to fall madly in love with me, could I?

"Good." Catherine gave me a real smile. One that lit up her eyes and made her look like her mom. "I'm glad we've sorted that out."

I could hardly believe my ears. I mean, I'd been willing to date this girl as a favour when she was a complete no-hoper. And now that she looked half-way decent, she didn't want to date me. Unbelievable. I just couldn't get my head round it. Cue total and complete collapse of the Aidan Douglas Masterplan.

"So," I ground out through gritted teeth, mortified through to my inner being. "Are we going to this stupid dance or not?"

CHAPTER SEVEN

When Catherine and I eventually arrived at the school disco, we created as much of a stir as if one of the Royal Family had turned up in the nude. The disco was being held in the school hall, but even before we'd gotten in there, there were plenty of kids milling about in the yard, and in the corridors. Their eyes nearly fell out of their heads when they saw Catherine and me walking along together.

"Everybody's staring at us," Catherine whispered in my ear as we queued up outside the hall to pay.

"Yeah," I said shortly. I still hadn't got over Catherine claiming she didn't fancy me. In fact, it was buggin' me somewhat seriously. Come on, be honest. What's wrong with me? Go on, give me the whole deal. I can take it. See? I knew you wouldn't be able to think of anything.

"Still, I suppose you're used to being stared at," Catherine remarked as we shuffled closer to the head of the queue. "What with you being so good-looking and smart and funny, et cetera, et cetera."

"Yeah," I said even more shortly. *How could this girl not be attracted to me?*

"Must be a problem for you."

"What?" I stared at her, bewildered.

"I said, it must be a problem for you, having to carry that oversized head of yours around all the time." Catherine pulled her purse out of her pocket, and looked up at me innocently. I goggled at her.

"You sayin' I'm conceited?"

"Well, maybe just a teeny weeny bit." Catherine was laughing up at me openly now. I stared at her for a second or two, and then I couldn't help starting to smile myself. She sure had me nailed. OK, I admit it. If I have got a fault, I am a bit vain. OK, more than a bit. A lot. Thing was, I wasn't used to being teased about it like this. And especially not by a *girl*. But strangely enough, I didn't really mind.

"Hey, put your purse away," I said sternly as we reached the entrance door, where Mrs Bradley of the concrete hairstyle was collecting money. "I asked you along, so I'm paying."

At least I hoped I was. I hunted desperately through every single pocket of my jacket and jeans while Mrs Bradley clicked her tongue impatiently. Come on, Jo-Jo, I prayed desperately, don't fail me now. Then my hand closed over a pile of coins in my back pocket, and thankfully I pulled them out.

"Er, how much?"

"A pound for the two of you." I stared helplessly at the heap of strange-looking money in my hand. Rolling her eyes, Mrs B. leaned over and picked out a yellow coin. "Lemonade and Coca-cola on sale at the back of the hall, keep away from the classrooms, no drink to be brought in from outside, no smoking."

"Jeez, they sure go all-out to make sure we have a good time," I muttered with somewhat heavy sarcasm as we went through into the darkened hall. There were plenty of kids in there already, dancing to a thumping beat that was shaking the photos of grim-looking ex-principals that hung on the walls. One of the sixth-formers was leaping about enthusiastically on the stage, spinning the discs, and surrounded by flashing lights. There were several hundred teachers wandering about too, just to make sure nobody broke the rules and enjoyed themselves too much.

"Yeah, you're right. It's pretty grim," Catherine yelled in my ear over the loud music.

"Serves you right for forcing me to come with you."

I shot her a sour look, but she just smiled sweetly at me. It looked as if Catherine Lucas didn't even care that she'd just knocked back the best-lookin' boy in the whole school. What was this babe's problem, I thought, frustrated. I'd been so totally confident that she was going to fall gratefully into my arms like a ripe peach and let me sort out all her troubles, no sweat. But instead, jeez, was I going to have some explaining to do to Jo-Jo when I got back Up There tonight. I bit my lip. If I didn't figure some way out of this mess, I might even be taken off the Lucas case.

"Hi, Aidan." Daniel Greene appeared out of the darkness and came towards us. I didn't recognize him at first. He looked different out of school uniform. Better-looking. Not quite in my league though. "Thought you'd decided not to come."

"Hi, Dan, how ya doin'?" I said grumpily. "Hey, you know Catherine, don't you?"

"Er, yeah." Daniel's mouth fell open. He stared so hard at Catherine, I got a bit annoyed. So I gave him what I hoped was a discreet nudge in the ribs.

"Ow!"

"Sorry, my arm slipped." I fixed him with a sour glance. But it still didn't stop him staring at Catherine.

"Did you get the lecture from Bradley at the door?" he said, talking to me but looking at Catherine.

"Yeah, we did." Catherine started giggling, and both Daniel and I watched her in fascination. It was amazing how different she looked from the tired, depressed, downtrodden girl we knew so well. "Now remember, children, no kissing, no drinking, no smoking, and *definitely* no fun!"

It was Mrs B. to the life. Daniel and I cracked up.

"That's excellent," I said, impressed. I'd always had a real soft spot for girls who could make me laugh. "Got any more like that?"

"I do a mean Mr Baxter," Catherine said, looking shy but pleased.

"Go on then."

"Ahem!" Catherine cleared her throat, and pulled her face into a ferocious, Baxter-type frown. "Anyone who breaks a test-tube will be boiled in sulphuric acid over a hot bunsen burner, and then hung on the lab door as a warning to other pupils!"

Daniel and I collapsed with laughter. Boy,

was this girl full of surprises. You know what – and this is a very big deal here – I was actually beginning to like her. A lot. And from the way Daniel was looking at her, he was thinking the very same thing. I frowned. I didn't need him muscling in on my territory. I opened my mouth quickly to ask Catherine if she wanted to dance, but before I could get the words out, a hand closed over my arm with a grip of steel.

"Aidan. Hi." It was Emma Freeman. Lookin' good in a skin-tight purple dress. "Like to dance with me?"

"I…" Weird. Very weird. A beautiful blonde was practically dragging me on to the dance floor, and I was hesitating. I looked at Catherine, but she didn't say anything to stop me. She didn't even look jealous, for Pete's sake.

"Go on, Aidan," she said airily. "I'll stay and talk to Daniel."

As Emma Freeman took my hand and led me away, I almost broke my neck in half, twisting round to look back at Daniel and Catherine. They'd forgotten about me already, and were laughing about something or other, their heads bent close together. I seethed inwardly. What did that schmuck Greene think he was doing? He'd better keep his dirty little hands off Catherine or else.

"It's nice to have a chance to get to know you at last, Aidan," Emma Freeman was cooing as we swayed about in the middle of the crowd on the dance floor. "How are you settling in?"

"No. Yes. I mean, fine." I had to bob up and down like a demented frog to try and catch a glimpse of Daniel and Catherine at the side of the hall. They were still chatting away happily. Jeez, what were they finding to talk about all this time, I wondered furiously.

"Aidan!" There was a sharp, shrill edge to Emma's voice as she yelled my name in my ear. I guessed that she'd been speaking to me, and I hadn't taken any notice.

"Er, sorry." The record finished, and I breathed a silent sigh of relief. "Thanks for the dance." I shot away at the speed of light, but not before I'd caught a glimpse of Emma Freeman's face, brick-red with fury. It sure didn't go with her purple dress, let me tell you.

I headed over to where Daniel and Catherine were standing, with a determined gleam in my eye. Only to pull up somewhat sharply when I realized that they'd both vanished. It didn't take me too long to locate them though. They'd moved into the middle of the dance floor, and were getting on down together to the music.

My blood began to overheat pretty seriously as I stood at the side watching them. Hey, Catherine was supposed to be with me, wasn't she? So how come she was kissing up to Daniel Greene? Maybe Daniel's more her type than you are, suggested a nasty little voice at the back of my mind. Come off it, willya, I argued back. Dan was a nice kid, but compared with me he had the looks and personality of a dead insect. On a scale of 1 - 10, I was an eleven and he was a zero. It was a case of a man versus a mouse. A prince versus a peasant. The President of the United States versus a bum. James Dean versus Stan Laurel. The only advantage that Daniel Greene had over me was that he wasn't dead.

The record finished. Catherine glanced over, caught my eye and waved at me. I waved back, my face breaking into a grin, and waited for her to come over and join me. Eat dirt, Danny boy. It was my turn now.

Music blared out. And with hardly a pause for breath Daniel and Catherine had started dancing again. My jaw hit the floor. Hey, you guys, what about me? They'd barely done me the honour of giving me a second glance. OK, just for that, I could feel a major, major sulk coming on. Furiously I spun round, and stomped off to the men's room. If they wanted me, they could come and find me. Although from the way they were laughing and chatting away so damn happily with each other, they probably wouldn't have noticed if I'd blasted my way out of the school hall in a space shuttle.

The washroom was empty. I slouched over to the long mirror fixed to the wall, and stared at myself critically. C'mon, Ade, I said silently, what's wrong with you, you jerk? So Lucas doesn't go for you. Big deal. Out of thousands and thousands of babes in the world, one doesn't want to know. It wasn't a problem. Hey, if I really turned on the charm, I could probably even change her mind.

I still felt lousy. I turned the faucet full on, bent over and washed my face in the cool water. It was when I looked up in the mirror again that I nearly spontaneously combusted with shock.

"Aaaaargh!"

For one terrible moment I thought I'd turned into a hippy. Then I sussed. Instead of my reflection in the glass, I was staring straight at Jo-Jo.

"What you doin' there, for Pete's sake!" I yelled wildly. "You almost scared me to death!"

"You should be so lucky, man." Jo-Jo waved

93

at me. "Don't panic, I'm not really here. I'm, like, a hologram."

"You're, like, a moron," I hissed, shooting a nervous glance over my shoulder at the washroom door. "Somebody might come in any minute!"

"Cool it, man. They won't be able to see me. They'll just see you, like, talking to your own reflection in the mirror, that's all."

"Oh, so they'll just think I'm a real weirdo then. Fine," I gibed sulkily. "What're you doin' here anyway?"

"Well, why do you think, man?" Jo-Jo shook his head sadly at me. "To see if we can, like, salvage anything from this disaster. I mean, your masterplan has turned out pretty catastrophic all round, know what I mean?"

"OK, OK," I broke in irritably. "You don't have to rub it in."

"It's foolproof, you said. Catherine Lucas is bound to fall for me pretty damn hard, you said."

"OK!!" I yelled furiously. "So things have gone a bit wrong."

"A bit, man!"

"Look, just stop hasslin' me, OK?" I ran a hand through my hair in utter frustration. "Can I help it if Catherine Lucas is one peculiar babe?"

"Hey, mind your lip, man!" Jo-Jo threw me a black look. "That's our client you're badmouthin' here."

"So what happens now?" I asked, feeling more than a touch apprehensive. Was this the end of Aidan Douglas, Fledgeling Guardian Angel? "Am I off the case or what?"

"Hey, mellow out, man," Jo-Jo said soothingly. "All we've got to do is come up with a brand-new strategy, that's all. We'll talk about it later when you come back Up Here."

"OK." I felt a bit better for knowing I wasn't going to be hauled back Up There and have my wrists slapped for screwing everything up. But not much. I still couldn't believe that the Lucas had turned my advances down flat. Who did the babe think she was? I mean, it wasn't as if she had guys beatin' a path to her door –

"Cheer up, man," Jo-Jo said kindly. "It hasn't all been, like, a total disaster. At least you've found Catherine a dude she does like."

I looked at him, bewildered.

"I've what?"

"That Daniel Greene guy. Great move, Aidan, gettin' them together like that. They seem to be hittin' it off real good."

"You've got to be kidding!" I scowled

furiously at Jo-Jo in the mirror. "Catherine ain't interested in a jerk like Daniel Greene!"

"Hey, why're you so uptight all of a sudden, man?" Jo-Jo gave me a suspicious look. "You ain't takin' all this too personally, are you?"

I frowned.

"What d'you mean, too personally?"

"You're not gettin' emotionally involved with Catherine Lucas, are you, man?" Jo-Jo's eyes bored into mine. "Because if you are, you'd be off this case quicker than you can say knockin' on heaven's door."

"Emotionally involved? With The Lucas? Sure, I'm crazy about the girl". I gave him a sarcastic smile. "C'mon, Jo-Jo. Credit me with some taste."

"Uh-oh, someone's coming." Jo-Jo began to fade rapidly from the mirror, starting with his waist and working upwards. "Gotta go. We'll talk later about where we go from here, OK, kid?"

The door opened, and a couple of guys came in, just before Jo-Jo's head and the gross purple headband disappeared. They didn't seem to notice though. Meanwhile I dragged myself away from the mirror, feeling even lousier than when I'd walked in five minutes ago. OK, so I was going to get a second chance to bring The

Lucas into line, but that wasn't the point. I'd screwed up, and I didn't like it. Not one tiny little bit.

When I got back into the hall, though, things improved. Catherine was standing at the side of the dance floor on her own. No sign of Daniel (The Predator) Green. I whizzed over to her at speed. Alone at last.

"Hi."

"Oh, hi, where did you get to?" Catherine turned round to smile at me. So she *had* noticed I was missing. That was something, I guess.

"I just went to the men's room. Where's Dan?"

"Gone to get some drinks." Catherine flapped a hand in front of her face. "It's like an oven in here."

Cue the-faster-than-the-speed-of-light-Aidan-Douglas-counter-manouevre.

"How about if we go outside for some air?" I suggested casually.

"What about Daniel?"

"Oh, he'll come and find us," I assured her airily. Not if I saw him first though. Daniel Greene was obviously someone who had no concept of that old two's-company-three's-a-pain-in-the-butt-type-thing. "Anyway, we'll be real quick. Come on."

The exit doors that led out into the back of the schoolyard had been left unlocked. I ushered Catherine towards them, hoping that Daniel hadn't spotted us leaving. We went outside into the dark, cool night air. It was calm and peaceful out there after the heat and the noise inside.

"Looks like there's some pretty serious necking going on out here," I commented brightly, looking round at the entwined couples in the shadows. I was feeling sort of embarrassed. Don't ask me why. "Let's hope Mrs B. doesn't come snooping round and march them all off to the school dungeons."

"Oh, Mrs Bradley's not so bad," Catherine said with a smile. "As old bats go."

Silence for thirty seconds. Forty seconds. Fifty seconds. A minute. Being surrounded by all these kissin' couples was making me nervous. Frantically I racked my brains for something to say.

"Have you forgiven me yet for making you come out with me tonight?"

"Oh, that." Catherine looked at me with those amazing eyes. "I suppose so. I haven't been out for so long, I'd forgotten what having a good time meant."

"I guess you don't get out much, do you?" I

said sympathetically. "What with your mom, and your job and all—"

"How do you know about my job?" she broke in, looking panic-stricken.

"I, er, just happened to be passing the Bigshot Burger Bar the other night," I said hastily, "and I saw you waiting tables."

"You won't say anything to anyone, will you, Aidan?" Catherine was staring at me pleadingly. "I'm not supposed to work the hours I do. If the authorities found out, I'd have to stop."

"I won't tell anyone," I promised, feeling as though I was breaking up inside. Jeez, to be in such a bad way that you had to work illegally in a place like the Bigshot Burger Bar and be grateful for it. It made me want to spit. "Do you have to do it? It looked like a real sordid dive."

"We need the money." Catherine's face was closing up into the tight, pinched look I knew so well.

"Look, I don't wanna pry—"

"You could've fooled me."

"—but are you sure you've tried every other which way to get cash?"

"Oh, you mean have I put a stocking over my head and tried to rob a bank yet?"

Catherine snapped sarcastically. "No, I'm saving that as my last option."

"Aw, come on, Cath. I'm only trying to help." I reached out, took hold of her shoulders and pulled her round to face me. "You don't have to struggle through this thing on your own. There's people who can help you – charities, welfare, even the school – if only you'd swallow that damn pride of yours for five minutes. And what about your dad?" I remembered just in time that I wasn't supposed to know anything about her. "Can't he help out, wherever he is?"

"We don't need anything from him," Catherine snapped coldly. "He ran off with another woman and left us."

"All the more reason why he ought to be supporting you and your mom." I tightened my grip. "He owes you."

Her face pale with anger, Catherine tore herself away from me.

"Congratulations."

"What for?"

"You've just won first prize for being the most annoying and interfering person I've ever met, as well as the most conceited!" she spat at me. "I can cope without your so-called advice, thanks very much!"

"C'mon, Catherine, it ain't a crime to admit you're goin' under. And what about your mom?" I pressed on relentlessly. "She deserves a whole heap better than she's getting right now. If you won't do it for yourself, do it for her."

The mention of her mom made the hard expression on Catherine's face crumple into vulnerability.

"Do you always waltz into everyone's life and start ordering them around when you've only known them a week?" she muttered, turning away from me.

"Only when I care about them," I said urgently. "Think about it, willya. Just think about it."

"We'd better go back inside." Catherine carefully avoided answering me. But at least she hadn't blown me out again. Maybe, just maybe I'd got through to her. "Daniel must be looking for us."

"Hey, forget Daniel for just five seconds, OK?" I snapped, suddenly annoyed. "What's the deal between you two anyway?"

Catherine threw me a haughty stare.

"What do you mean?"

"You know what I mean. Is he coming on to you?"

"It wouldn't be any of your business if he

was!" Catherine retorted, her eyes lighting up challengingly. "What's the matter with you? Are you trying to run my love life as well?"

"Yeah, I am," I said shortly. "He ain't the right guy for you."

"Oh, and you are, I suppose?" she flung at me, her eyes shimmering with rage.

"Well, yeah, I happen to think I'm a better bet than Mr Personality in there!" I jerked my thumb contemptuously at the school hall. "What's he got that I haven't?"

"Nothing." Catherine retorted coldly, squaring up to me. "I just happen to prefer nice, ordinary boys like Daniel Greene to big-headed, vain, arrogant, conceited prats like you."

"Hey, I'm not that bad!" I protested, taken aback. "Am I?"

"You're not exactly the most modest person I've ever met," Catherine said promptly. We were practically nose to nose now, glaring at each other.

"Gee, thanks a lot." I snapped sarcastically. "You're too kind. So you don't want to date me, huh?"

"You're catching on quick." Catherine put her hands on her hips and glared at me. "I'd rather go out with the Hunchback of Notre Dame."

"Oh yeah?" I was gettin' mad now. Really mad. "Betcha he can't kiss as good as I can."

I don't know what came over me, but it was then that I leaned over and kissed her. Kinda quick before she could object. Right on the lips. Her mouth was soft and warm, and she didn't try to push me away. I guess she was just too surprised. But the kiss only lasted about two and a half seconds anyway. Almost the moment our mouths met, there was a clap of ear-splitting thunder, followed by a vivid streak of lightning cutting the sky in half. And then the rain poured down on us like a river from heaven.

I chewed nervously at my lip as I ran back into the hall for cover behind Catherine. Somehow I got the feeling I was in trouble Up There. Deep trouble. Because over the booming noise of the thunder I could hear Jo-Jo's furious voice in my ear.

"Get ready to beam up in ten seconds, Douglas. You've just made a big, big mistake."

CHAPTER EIGHT

"But, Jo-Jo, if you'll just let me explain."

"Boy, oh boy, have you screwed up this time, Aidan." I hadn't managed to get a word in edgeways yet because Jo-Jo was too busy pacing his cloud, groaning and holding his hairy head in his hands. I stared down at my feet, feeling pretty damn uneasy. Something told me I was going to have to put on an Oscar-winning performance, and then some, to get myself out of this one. "Did I warn you about gettin' emotionally involved with Catherine Lucas, or did I warn you?"

"Jo-Jo, I am not emotionally involved with Catherine Lucas!" I hoped I was managing to sound casual, because my stomach was tying itself into agonised reef-knots. I was in it up to my neck this time. "Look, relax, willya? It was only one stupid little kiss."

"One stupid little kiss!" Jo-Jo screeched in an outraged voice. "D'you realize you could be taken off the case for this? I told you, man, when you went down there the first time, remember? No physical contact except in the line of duty! And this sure wasn't in the line of duty. The chick doesn't even dig you. She said so herself."

"Thanks for reminding me," I muttered grimly under my breath.

"This is serious, dude. Guardian Angels can't go around kissin' LPs without a darned good reason, man, and you ain't given me one yet." Jo-Jo advanced on me, looking pretty damn threatening for an old hippy. "Come on, admit it. You kissed Catherine Lucas because you're fallin' for the chick."

"Falling for Lucas? Please." I burst into derisory laughter. "Give me a break, Jo-Jo. No way."

"Sez you." Jo-Jo folded his arms and stared hard at me. "C'mon, man, tell the truth. You're dead jealous of that Daniel Greene kid because Catherine likes him better than she likes you."

I turned seven different shades of red.

"I'm *not* jealous of that jerk Greene!"

"You're jealous, man."

"I am not!"

"You are so too, man."

"Look, I'm not falling for Lucas and I'm not jealous of Daniel Greene, period!" I howled furiously. "For a start, Lucas isn't my type. I mean, you've seen the kind of babes I used to date. Do you really think I'd fall for somebody like Catherine Lucas? I mean, who cares if she doesn't want to go out with me? Who cares if she wants to go out with that bonehead Greene? I ain't gonna lose any sleep over it."

"Me thinks the dude does, like, protest too much," Jo-Jo said sarcastically. "So c'mon then, man. If you ain't fallin' for the girl, why did you kiss her? Just to, like, pass the time?"

"Yes, I mean, no," I stammered, feeling pretty confused myself. I'd really blown things this time, but I couldn't give up now. The thought of not being allowed to go back down to earth again was slowly killing me inside. And it was all because of one kiss. One lousy kiss that hadn't even meant anything. I wasn't really sure myself why I'd gone and kissed Catherine Lucas out of the blue, but I mean, it wasn't as if I had the hots for the girl or anything, was it? In fact, now that I had time to think about it, it was pretty insulting of Jo-Jo to accuse me of having a thing about The Lucas at all. I mean, Aidan Douglas, A-Grade Good-Looker and Girl-bait Extraordinaire, did not get involved with average-type babes like Catherine Lucas. Not even if they had great personalities. Not even if they could make a guy laugh. Not even if their eyes shimmered like the sea in the sun when they got really mad...

Hastily I pushed the memory right to the back of my mind. "Jo-Jo, if you'd just give me a chance to explain."

"Explain away." Jo-Jo smiled sourly at me. "This I've got to hear."

I ran my hand through my hair, my brain whirring round like crazy. This was going to be tricky. I had to have, in Jo-Jo-speak, "a darned good reason, man", for steppin' outta line like I had done. And guess what? Yep, I didn't have one. So I was just going to have to make up a pretty convincing story, and fast. My future visits to earth depended on it.

"Look, Jo-Jo." I put on my Aidan Douglas Special Sincere Expression. The one I'd always used when I was promising anxious fathers that I'd have their daughters home by ten-thirty sharp. "That kiss didn't happen because I'm attracted to Catherine Lucas. It was all part of my plan."

"Plan? What plan?" Jo-Jo repeated scornfully. "Like, pull the other one, man."

"No, really, Jo-Jo." I was desperately trying not to sound desperate. "You remember my masterplan?"

"You mean the one where you were goin' to waltz into school, sweep Catherine off her feet and sort out her life in, like, the twinkling of an eye?" Jo-Jo said with heavy sarcasm. "Yeah, I remember, man. And it turned out to be a real bummer."

"Yeah, but this is the Aidan Douglas Masterplan Mark 2," I broke in hastily. Jeez, could I pull this off or not? "I made a few changes."

"The Aidan Douglas Masterplan Mark 2," Jo-Jo's voice was heavy with sarcasm. "Tell me more, man."

"OK…" I took a deep breath. Hey, this making-everything-up-as-I-go-along-type-thing had always been one of my specialities. And I'd never needed to think as quickly and as clearly as I did now. "Picture the scene."

Jo-Jo buried his head in his hands and groaned.

"Oh, man, I think I've heard this somewhere before."

"Just give me a coupla minutes, Jo-Jo," I said urgently. "Like I said, picture the scene. One girl without a life. Two guys both crazy about her, fightin' it out to get a date with her. That ol' eternal love triangle. Passion. Romance. Drama. Excitement with a capital E. And Catherine

Lucas as the star of the whole damn show."

Jo-Jo stared at me, bewildered.

"I don't get it, man."

"C'mon, Jo-Jo, think about it. What could be better for a babe's ego than havin' *two* guys fightin' over her?"

"Two guys?"

"Me and Daniel Greene," I said impatiently. "Look, I figured it all out last night. That's why I kissed Catherine. The plan is I pretend I'm so crazy about her, I won't take no for an answer, even though she's knocked me back once. And I make out like I'm real jealous of Daniel Greene, because he's obviously got the hots for Catherine himself. Result: a Lurve Triangle that's gonna get everyone in the whole school talkin'. Catherine Lucas gets not one but two guys chasin' after her, making her feel pretty important, and givin' her self-confidence a turbo-charge. By the time I've finished with her, she'll be a different babe altogether." I looked eagerly at Jo-Jo. "That's the Masterplan Mark 2. What do you think?"

Jo-Jo started pacing up and down again.

"You shoulda cleared it with us first, man." He frowned. "You can't just go round changing the rules whenever you feel like it."

"I know, I know," I broke in quickly. "I

won't do it again. I promise."

"And that kiss, man."

"Like I said, I was acting, Jo-Jo. I mean, Catherine and Daniel have both got to believe that I've really got a thing about her for this one to work." I shrugged my shoulders nonchalantly. "I was pretty damn convincing, wasn't I?"

"Yeah. Very convincing." Jo-Jo threw me a suspicious look, and I had to steel myself not to blush.

"So what do you think?" I asked hastily. "Is it a good idea, or is it a good idea?"

Jo-Jo carried on pacing up and down. I breathed hard, waiting for him to make up his mind at his usual tortoise-like pace.

"Yeah," he said at last. "I reckon you've probably got something there. Havin' two guys runnin' round in circles for her could do wonders for Catherine's self-confidence. Yeah. I like it, man."

My knees trembled with relief. I'd done it. I'd really gone and pulled it off.

"What about The Boss?" I asked, trying not to sound too triumphant. "Do you think he'll go for it? D'you think he'll keep me on the case?"

"Oh, The Boss had already decided to give

you another chance, anyway, man." Jo-Jo gave me an innocent look. "He reckons the Lucas case is, like, at a critical point, and he doesn't want to rock the boat."

"Well, gee, thanks for makin' me sweat all that time," I snapped furiously. "Why didn't you just tell me everything was cool right away?"

"Because you deserved to sweat for a bit, man," Jo-Jo said sternly. He pulled his clipboard out from under his arm, and scribbled down a few notes. "OK. Let's give this idea of yours a try. You go back down to earth on Monday morning, and, like, play the jealous Other Guy. Sorry I had a go at you back there, man. But you have to admit, that kiss between you and Catherine looked pretty realistic."

"Hey, forget it," I said airily. "As long as The Boss is happy with the job I'm doin'. I mean, He must know for sure that there's nothing going on between me and The Lucas, right?"

"Right." Jo-Jo stared at me hard for a few moments. For no apparent reason that I could think of, I turned bright red, and looked down at my feet. "The Boss knows everything, Aidan, man," Jo-Jo went on softly. "Just remember that."

Monday morning. Jeez, was I glad to hot-rod it back down to earth again after the weekend. I was even pretty glad to get back into school uniform, and feel that stupid tie round my neck. Every time I thought about how close I'd come to screwing up and never being allowed back down here again, I turned cold inside. And all because I'd happened to kiss Catherine Lucas for a couple of seconds. Big deal. Still, I'd managed to talk my way out of a very tricky situation in my usual inimitable style, I thought smugly. Coming up with the Masterplan Mark 2 at about five seconds' notice had been a stroke of genius – apart from the fact that I was now stuck with the somewhat dubious task of pretending to slug it out with Daniel Greene for Catherine Lucas's favours. It would be the first time in my whole existence, dead or alive, that I'd ever had to fight over a babe with another guy. The shame of it. I didn't feel quite so smug either as I wondered what would happen if Catherine decided she preferred the Greene Wimp to yours truly. The mere thought of me, Aidan Douglas, being humiliated and mortified in front of the whole school was enough to make me want to throw up. Turned down in favour of a jerk like DG? I'd rather have all my body hair tweezed out with a pair of pliers.

Nope. I just couldn't let that happen.

The first thing I noticed when I appeared on the sidewalk outside the school was Daniel (Personality of a Limp Lettuce) Greene standing by the gates, and staring up and down the street, as if he was looking for someone pretty special. He was so engrossed he didn't notice me materializing right behind him. In fact, I doubt if he'd have noticed if The Boss Man Himself had arrived in person, he was so intent on staring into the distance. And I didn't need three guesses to work out who he was looking for. My lip curled contemptuously, Elvis-style. This guy was *so* obvious.

"Hi, Dan." I leaned over and tapped him on the shoulder. "You waiting for somebody?"

Daniel leapt about ten feet into the air, and spun round. Hey, if there'd been an award for The Guiltiest Look of The Year, this guy would've walked it.

"Oh, er... hi, Aidan." A bright red blush spread rapidly over his face, starting at his neck and working upwards. "Um, no, I'm not waiting for anybody in particular."

"Oh yeah?" I raised my eyebrows at him. This guy sure needed some lessons in the great art of the little white lie. He couldn't have fooled a ten-month-old baby. "If you say so."

"So what happened to you at the disco on Friday?" Dannyboy also desperately needed a lesson or two in the equally great art of subtly changing the subject. "One minute you were there, the next you'd disappeared."

"Yeah. And I bet you were real pleased about that," I said sarcastically. "Weren't you?"

"What?"

"OK, Dan." I faced him head-on, and stared him right between the eyes. "You can stop messin' me about right now. I know you're waiting for Catherine Lucas."

Daniel turned even redder.

"So what if I am?" he said defensively. "There's no law against it, is there?"

"Don't try and be smart, Greene," I said tightly. "It doesn't suit you. You've got the hots for Catherine Lucas, haven't you? C'mon. Admit it."

"So what?" Daniel squared up to me, and stared right back. Which surprised me somewhat seriously. I'd always had him down as a bit of a wimp. No. A lot of a wimp. Guess I'd been wrong. "Is it any of your business?"

"Yeah. I reckon it is my business." I held his gaze steadily. Some of the other kids who were on their way into school stopped to stare curiously at us. "Catherine ain't interested in you. So back off, willya? Don't stick your nose in where it isn't wanted."

"She seemed pretty interested in me at the disco," Daniel snapped back. "Until you went and stuck your big fat nose in."

"Hey, it was me who brought her to that stupid dance, wasn't it?" I said indignantly. "Back where I come from, that means that the girl's with you, and other guys don't muscle in. Guess you lot over here don't have the same sort of rules."

"Yeah, we do." Daniel glared at me. "But Catherine told me you and her were only mates."

I almost choked. So The Lucas was going around telling everybody she didn't have a thing for me, huh? I was mortified.

"I'm warning you, Dan." I moved towards him. I was acting the part of Catherine's jealous suitor so well, I was somewhat seriously losing my cool. For real. And there was now a large crowd of fellow-pupils gathering around us, which didn't help. "You don't stand a chance with Catherine Lucas. So stay away."

Greene glared at me.

"You're only saying that because you fancy her yourself."

"Yeah." I spoke with deadly intensity. "I

do." Pretty convincing, huh? For somebody who's just pretending, I mean.

"So does she fancy you then, Douglas, or what?" Daniel stared challengingly at me. "She didn't seem too impressed with you at the disco. Word is, she called you a vain, arrogant, conceited prat."

The crowd of kids standing around us started to giggle. I almost burst a blood vessel.

"D'you seriously think any girl's gonna look twice at a dork like you with me around?"

"What I seriously think is that a big-headed Yank like you needs a couple of hard punches right on the nose." Greene clenched his fists threateningly. Whew! I didn't know the guy had it in him.

"Just try it," I snarled through gritted teeth. The circle of kids around us shuffled in a few inches closer, and started chanting gleefully "Fight! Fight!"

"So we're going to fight then, are we?" I lifted an eyebrow at Dannyboy. He shrugged.

"It's one way of sorting things out, I suppose."

"Guess so. OK, I'm in." I started to take off my jacket. "And the loser butts out of Catherine's life, right?"

"Right."

OK, I know that a boxing match with another guy over a girl probably wasn't standard Guardian Angel behaviour. But hey, I was only faking it, wasn't I? Anyway, I couldn't back out now, not with half the school watching. This Love Triangle thing had gone public in a big way. And I didn't have time to rush off to the john, and get permission from the hippy hologram. So I threw my jacket on the ground, and loosened my tie.

"Would you two mind telling me what you're playing at?"

Daniel and I both gulped audibly, and spun round. Catherine had pushed her way through the tight circle of kids around us, and was standing right there in the ring with us, her arms folded. For at least thirty seconds there was complete silence as everyone goggled at her, including me and Daniel. She was lookin' OK. Better than OK. In fact, she looked so different from the way she'd been that very first day I met her, she was like another person. Her school uniform was still a bit of a mess, but she'd obviously made an effort to tidy it up. She was wearing a different sweater that wasn't new, but at least it didn't have any holes in the elbows, and she'd fixed the falling-down hem on her skirt. Her legs were not bad. Pretty

117

good, in fact. And she'd pulled her hair up into a high ponytail tied with a red ribbon.

As Catherine's eyes briefly met mine, I began to feel seriously alarmed. Suddenly I wasn't a well guy. My whole body was shaking, my heartbeat was erratic and I was getting hot and cold flushes. It felt like influenza. But I'd been fine until a few minutes ago. I just couldn't understand it. Anyway, whatever it was, it had got my tongue. I couldn't say a word. Neither could Daniel. He was standing beside me, opening and closing his mouth like a fish with laryngitis.

"I think you two had better come with me, and we'll have a little talk," Catherine said calmly. She turned round and walked out of the circle, and the open-mouthed kids moved aside to right and left to let her through. It was like the parting of the Red Sea. It was awesome. Meanwhile, Daniel and I shuffled along obediently behind her like a pair of naughty kindergarten kids. We followed her through the gates and into the schoolyard, and Catherine didn't say a word. It wasn't until we were out of sight of the other kids behind the canteen that she stopped and turned to face us.

"Would one of you mind telling me what all that was about?" she enquired coolly.

Daniel and I both looked down at our feet.

"Nothing," we said in unison.

"Don't give me that. I heard my name mentioned a couple of times, so I think I'm entitled to know what's going on." Catherine looked from me to Dan, and back again. I don't know about Dan, but I'd never felt such an out-and-out jerk in my life. "What were you fighting about?"

There was silence for a couple of minutes while I waited for Daniel to answer, and he waited for me to do the same thing. In the end we both said it together in a squeaky voice.

"You."

"Me?" Catherine's eyes widened. "You were fighting over me?" She looked from one to the other of us for about thirty seconds without saying a word. Then she started to laugh. Daniel and I glanced at each other, bewildered.

"What're you laughing for?" I snapped, aggrieved. Jeez, I'd been prepared to risk permanent injury to my somewhat seriously attractive face on this babe's behalf, and all she could do was laugh.

"Because you two are such a pair of prats." Catherine shook her head at us, still giggling. "Look, you'd better work things out and make up, OK? Because I'm not going to be friends

119

with you two idiots unless you sort things out." She spun round on her heel, and walked off, leaving Daniel and me with our mouths dropping open. This woman was seriously unbelievable. Most other girls I'd known would have turned the whole thing into a big emotional drama. And she'd just stood there and laughed her head off.

"What a girl." Daniel was staring dreamily after her. "She's unbelievable."

"Yeah…" I watched Catherine march off across the schoolyard without once looking back. My legs were wobbling, and my heart was thumping away like a big bass drum. That damn 'flu bug again. Jeez, I didn't even know you could catch 'flu once you were dead. "She's kinda individual, I'll say that for her."

"So, no hard feelings, mate?" Daniel held out his hand. So did I, and we shook. "I suppose we've just got to wait for Catherine to decide who she wants to go out with."

"I guess so. May the best guy win, huh?" I grinned at him in a friendly kind of way. But hey, we all know who the best guy is here, don't we? No contest. And OK, OK, you lot out there can keep your hair on. I know I'm only pretending to be madly in love with Catherine, but let's face it - that doesn't mean to say I want to come second in the boyfriend stakes to a jerk like Daniel Greene, does it? I mean, a guy's got his pride. Especially now that virtually the whole school knew we were both chasing her. So I reckoned I was entitled, for the sake of my reputation as an Irresistible Hunk, to do my best to make Catherine like me better than she liked him. OK, so the girl had knocked me back once. OK, so she claimed that she didn't have the hots for me one bit. But Aidan Douglas, The King of the Chat-Up Line, was out to change her mind. I was pretty damn determined to make Catherine Lucas fall crazily in love with me after all, just to salvage some of my wounded pride. But hey, you lot, not a word to Jo-Jo, OK? This has got to be our little secret.

CHAPTER NINE

Jeez. Did the Aidan Douglas Masterplan Mark 2 work like the proverbial dream or what. Catherine might have thought me and Dannyboy Greene fighting over her was a joke, but it had sure done the trick. In the space of a single schoolday The Lucas had gone from a downtrodden nobody without a life, to the Glamorous Heroine of the Fourth Form. She'd become the girl who had two guys about to fight to the death over her. A femme fatale. A Mata Hari. Suddenly, she was a Desirable Babe.

The change was awesome. Ever since Daniel and I had squared up to knock the innards out of each other that morning, nobody in the whole damn school had been able to talk about anything else. Everybody was dying to know what was going to happen next. Whom Catherine was going to choose, me or Daniel, and what was going to happen when one of us was jilted. The whole affair was rapidly taking on the dimensions of a soap opera. Some of the kids had even started to lay bets on the guy Catherine would choose. I was the 2–1 favourite. Naturally.

So I'd done it. I'd finally pulled it off. Finally begun to do something positive to put Catherine's life to rights. She was blossoming visibly under all the attention, and she was looking better and brighter-eyed and more confident by the second. She'd spent the whole day surrounded by the girls in our class, who were dying to find out the story behind the love triangle, and it looked like she might even make a few girlfriends. So after a pretty shaky start, I guess I could say that I'd earned my Guardian Angel's wings.

"I've gotta hand it to you, man." Jo-Jo was so impressed when I reported back to him that evening, he just couldn't stop smiling. "You've come good at last. OK, I, like, had my doubts about you," he slapped me enthusiastically on the back, "but you've really blown me away this time."

"Thanks." I tried to look modest. Something I'd always found particularly difficult. "Told you the Masterplan Mark 2 was foolproof, didn't I?"

"Yeah. But you said that about the Masterplan Mark 1."

"OK, OK. So we had a few temporary blips along the way," I said airily. "But I always knew I could see this one through."

"Yep, things are goin' groovy. Real groovy." Jo-Jo consulted the papers on his clipboard. "That was an ace idea of yours to have you and that Greene kid fightin' over Catherine like that. It's sure giving her just the boost she needed."

"All in a day's work." I shrugged my shoulders nonchalantly. Whew. What a damn smart guy I was. I'd pulled the Masterplan Mark 2 outta nothing to get myself out of a jam, and it had gone and worked perfectly.

"There's just one thing…" Jo-Jo looked up from his papers, and frowned at me.

"What?"

"Well, it's just a hint, man. Don't overdo the rivalry thing. Remember, you're only pretendin' to be part of this, like, eternal triangle."

"I know that," I said crossly. "But I've got to be realistic, haven't I? I mean, if I'm supposed to be competing with Greene for Catherine, I gotta compete."

"Yeah. True. But did you have to lock him in the john so you could be alone with Catherine at recess?"

I blushed.

"I didn't exactly lock him in," I muttered sheepishly. "I just sort of wedged a chair underneath the door handle. Anyway, he was the one who nearly trampled me underfoot so he could get a seat next to Catherine in class." I looked sourly down at the black and blue mark on my foot. "And I've got the bruise to prove it."

"Still, you got your own back, man, didn't you?" Jo-Jo raised his eyebrows at me. "I mean, you were the one who hid Daniel's history notes so he was late for class and got a detention at lunchtime. Leavin' you free to have a cosy lunch with Catherine all alone."

"Look, Jo-Jo, I'm playin' a part here!" I said snappishly. "If I want to be convincing, I've got to throw myself into it."

"Just don't throw yourself in too deep, man, that's all." Jo-Jo fixed me with a beady-eyed stare. "You're the one who can't win any which way. You'll be coming back Up Here, and it's Daniel who'll be left behind with Catherine. So don't get in over your head. You're just the stooge here. Remember that."

Remember it? I could hardly forget it, I thought bitterly, a sudden pain twisting my heart. After all, it was hard to forget that you were dead when everyone else around you down on earth was alive. But that didn't mean to say I was going to lie down and let Daniel Greene walk all over me. I mean, I wasn't going to let him snatch the girl away from under my nose just because I happened to be dead. And whatever Jo-Jo said, I was still secretly determined to make Catherine Lucas fall for me if it was the last thing I did. Which it probably would be. I was going to make sure, when it came to the crunch, that she chose me and not that Greene kid. I didn't care that I was dead and on a one-way ticket back Up Here, I just wanted to make sure I came out on top. My ego just wouldn't be able to take it otherwise. No other reason.

I'd thought a lot about the best way to get Catherine interested in me, and I'd come to the conclusion that the babe went for shy, sensitive, sincere guys. I guess it was a bit late for me to come over all shy and sensitive, huh? But at least I could do the sincerity thing pretty damn well. I was going to be more sincere than I'd ever been before. I was going to be so sincere, Catherine was going to have all her doubts about me blown away.

"What are you standing there with that stupid expression on your face for?"

Tuesday morning. I'd arrived down there before class to find Catherine on her own in the schoolyard. No sign of Daniel Greene. A great chance to start all that being-sincere-and-honest-type-thing. Trouble was, Catherine seemed less than impressed. She was frowning at me, and shaking her head. "You look like a secondhand car salesman."

Hastily I wiped the Sincere, You Can Trust Me, Honest John expression I'd been practising all night off my face.

"Thanks a lot," I snapped with a scowl. There the babe was, sittin' calmly on that damn wall, looking better than she had done for days. Here I was, the guy who was behind it all, and she still couldn't be nice to me. "Tell me one thing, huh? Why do you have to criticize me all the time?"

"Why are you always pretending to be something you're not?" Catherine shot back promptly. "Maybe we'd get on better if you just tried to be yourself for a change, instead of putting on an act."

I felt seriously aggrieved.

"Hey, that *was* me being myself. Bein' sincere."

"Yuk." Catherine pulled a face. "I think I preferred you when you were being a bighead."

I stared at her uncertainly. What was it about this babe? She seemed to have every one of my moves taped, right down to the last little detail. OK, then. Counter-manouevre. Let's try some real sincerity for a change.

"Sorry. I guess I was being a bit of a jerk." I looked straight into her eyes. "I was just tryin' to impress you."

"How do you work that one out?"

"I figured you went for the shy, sensitive, sincere type." I smiled ruefully. "That was my big Sincere Scene."

Catherine smiled back at me, and my insides unexpectedly flipped.

"Zero for style and zero for content."

"That bad, huh?" I shrugged. "Well, you can't blame a guy for trying."

"Even after what I told you on Friday night?" Catherine was looking at me with a curious expression in her green-blue eyes. "Remember? You asked me out and I told you we could be mates but nothing else."

"I guess I just can't take no for an answer." It was weird. There were plenty of screaming kids running round the yard, but at that moment the world seemed to have shrunk to me and Catherine Lucas staring intensely into each other's eyes, as if we were desperate to read each other's minds.

"I gathered that from the way you kissed me anyway," Catherine said dryly. She looked at me thoughtfully. "So why won't you take no for an answer, Aidan? Is it because you can't bear to be turned down by a girl? Any girl?" Her mouth curved into a gently mocking smile. "Or is it because you really like me?"

I gazed at her, my mind in a whirl of total confusion. This was honesty time. Real honesty. Raw honesty. So what did I say? I wasn't even sure about the answer to that one myself. Or was I? C'mon, Aidan, let's have the truth here. But would I be able to recognize the truth if it jumped up and bit me on the nose? Maybe. If it bit me hard enough. I opened my mouth, closed it and opened it again.

"I..."

"Hi, you two. All right?"

I shut my mouth again with a snap. If ever Daniel (Always One to Poke My Nose In Where It Ain't Required) Greene had ever turned up at a bad moment, this had to be the one. Speechless with rage, I threw him a look that would have destroyed him on the spot, if looks could kill. Just for a second there, Catherine and I had come really close to being as open and honest as we'd ever been with each other. We'd finally started to talk truthfully. Started to get to know each other. And this jerk had to come along and spoil it.

"Hello, Daniel." Catherine smiled at him, and I wanted to throttle the guy.

"Oh, by the way, Mrs Bradley's looking for you, Aidan." Daniel nodded at me. "She didn't say what about."

"OK," I said through gritted teeth. "I'll go and catch her now." No point in hanging around while Greene was on the scene. No chance of a heart-to-heart now. As I stalked furiously away, I threw a look back at Catherine over my shoulder. Our eyes met briefly, and I was so shaken up, I walked straight into one of the junior kids and almost flattened him. Hey, all this sincerity thing can make you feel real weird, y'know. Kinda high.

I went down the corridor to our classroom in a daze. Mrs B. was in there, pinning a poster to the pinboard. She spun round like a whirling dervish when I opened the door.

"What are you doing in here, Aidan?" she snapped. "You know the rules. You're not allowed inside until the bell goes."

"I got your message," I said hastily before she lunged across the room and lynched me.

"What message?" Mrs B. looked puzzled.

"The message that you wanted to see me–"
I stopped as she still looked bewildered. It
finally hit me. One up to Daniel Greene. And
like a jerk, I'd gone and fallen for it.

"I think somebody made a mistake," I said
grimly. "Sorry."

Mrs B. gave me a long, hard stare, then
decided to believe me.

"The bell's just about to go so you might as
well stay inside now anyway."

Angrily I grabbed the nearest chair, pulled it
roughly out and sat down on it with a thud.
Mrs B. raised an eyebrow at me, but she didn't
say anything. I was seething inwardly. First
Daniel Greene breaks up my cosy little chat
with Catherine, then he sends me off on a wild-
goose chase. The guy was a pain in the butt.

Grimly I started plotting my next move.
While I sat and thought about it, the poster Mrs
B. had been putting up on the pinboard caught
my eye.

"Our American Exchange students arrive
tomorrow, and to make them feel at home, this
Friday's disco will be an American-style Prom
Night!! So get out your blue suede shoes and
your bobby sox, and let's ROCK 'N'
ROLL!!!"

I had to smile. It sounded seriously dire. So

dire, it could be brilliant. And it would be even more brilliant if I could persuade Catherine to come to the prom with me as my date. One in the eye for Daniel Greene with the whole school looking on to witness his humiliating defeat would suit me just fine. I frowned as the bell rang. Revenge would be sweet. Real sweet. If only I could pull it off, and get Catherine to agree. But for once in my life, I wasn't sure if I could...

When Daniel came in for roll-call with Catherine, I glared significantly across the room at him. An I-know-you-set-me-up-Greene-so-just-you-wait kind of glare. Daniel just gave me a wide-eyed, innocent look in return that made my blood boil, and sat down quickly in the seat next to Catherine before I had a chance to stake my claim. I sat and seethed until the lesson bell rang, and when Mrs B. dismissed us, I caught up with him outside in the corridor.

"Very funny, Dannyboy," I ground out through my teeth. Catherine was still in the classroom, seeing Mrs B. about something, so I didn't have to pull any punches. "Don't think I'll fall for that old trick again, you jerk."

"What old trick?" Daniel smiled smugly at me. "Oh, you mean Mrs Bradley didn't want to see you after all? Sorry, mate, I must've made a mistake." He shrugged his shoulders. "Just like you made a mistake yesterday when you accidentally locked me in the loo."

I opened my mouth to hurl a couple of insults at him when Catherine came out of the classroom, and I shut it again.

"Come on, you two." Catherine hurried off down the corridor. "We're going to be late for maths."

Daniel and I both lunged forward to catch her up in a tangle of feet and schoolbags. It was me who tripped over the dangling laces of my Reeboks, and went flying.

"Ouch!" I sprawled on the grimy corridor floor, all the breath knocked out of my body. Catherine didn't even notice. She'd already gone shooting off around the corner.

"Sorry, mate." Daniel raced off after her, looking back to grin smugly at me over his shoulder. "It's just not your day, is it?"

No it wasn't, I thought grimly as I sat up and gingerly massaged my elbow. But the day wasn't over yet. Not by a long way.

Morning recess. Geography class had just finished, and we were all filing out into the schoolyard. I was trying to catch up with Daniel and Catherine but they were already halfway down the corridor while I was still hobbling out of the classroom. That jerk Greene had stepped on my other, formerly unbruised foot in the mad rush to grab the desk next to Catherine. I'd lost out. Again. Gritting my teeth, I put on a painful spurt, and caught up with them at the corner.

"Shall we go over to the canteen and get a couple of Cokes?" Daniel was saying.

"OK." Right at that minute Catherine turned round and saw me. "D'you want to come too, Aidan? We're just going to get a drink."

"Sure," I said airily, enjoying the disappointed look on Greene's face. Eat dirt, sucker. Your time is up.

Just then one of the other kids, a dopey-lookin' guy with blond hair sticking up in lethal spikes, slouched over to us.

"You Daniel Greene?" he enquired in a voice that broke about five times in the space of three words.

"Yeah." Daniel stared at him. "Why?"

"Mr Baxter wants to see you right away," squeaked the kid in a soprano key before he turned tenor again. "He's in the chemistry lab."

"Baxter?" Daniel looked bewildered. "What does the old prat want?"

The kid shrugged his shoulders.

"Dunno," he squeaked, and drifted away.

"I suppose I'd better go," Daniel said gloomily. "I'll catch up with you two later."

"OK." I put my hand on Catherine's arm. "How about we go and get those drinks, huh, Cath?"

It had been all too easy, I thought with a smug grin as I queued up at the school shop to buy the cokes. Some kids will do anything for what you guys call a fifty-pence piece. Including giving false messages to Daniel Greene – one up to me this time.

Still smiling to myself, I carried the coke cans across the schoolyard back to where I'd left Catherine sitting on one of the benches. As I went towards her, I noticed that she had her head bent over some sheets of schoolwork, and she was studying them real hard.

"Hey, relax, willya," I said lightly as I got back to her. "It's time for a break."

Catherine jumped as if she'd been shot, and quickly shoved the papers back into her schoolbag before I could get a good look at them. Now that I was close enough to see, they didn't look like school papers at all. I wondered what they were. And why she'd been so anxious for me not to see them.

"Thanks." Catherine reached out and took

one of the cans from me. "How did you get on in the maths test this morning?"

"OK, I guess." I stared at her schoolbag. What were those damn papers? The only thing I could think of was that they were love letters from Daniel Greene. Or maybe love poems. Yeah, he looked like just the kind of guy who'd write love poetry. I wandered lonely as a daffodil, and all that stuff. What a wimp. My blood boiled.

Catherine was staring at me.

"Is something the matter?"

"No. Nothing." I forced myself not to think about it. I had a few precious minutes alone with Catherine until Daniel (Wordsworth) Greene sussed that he'd been set up, and I wanted to make the most of them. "Cath, can I talk to you for a minute?"

"What're we doing at the moment? Climbing Mount Everest?"

"No, I mean really talk." I felt incredibly embarrassed, and cleared my throat a few times. "About this morning. What we were saying before that jerk – I mean, Daniel Greene – interrupted us."

"What about it?" Catherine looked at me levelly. Her eyes were givin' absolutely nothing away. Which made it all the harder for me to get the words out. I felt myself turning all shades of red.

"What you said about whether I was just interested in you because you knocked me back, or whether I really like you." I looked down at the floor, feeling like a kid on his first date. "I just wanted to – to tell you that I do like you. Really."

There was silence for a few minutes. I looked down at my feet, squirming horribly inside. I just couldn't understand myself. I mean, I'd done the whole routine: "I-love-you-you-look-beautiful-in-the-moonlight-I've-never-met-a-girl-like-you" thousands of times when I was alive. But somehow, just telling Catherine Lucas that I *liked* her was one of the hardest things I'd ever done. It wasn't even like I was swearing undying love for her or anything, was it? I just wanted to let the girl know that I thought she was OK. And by layin' all my cards on the table, I was hoping she'd admit that she thought I was OK too. More OK than Daniel Greene. I waited for her to speak with bated breath.

""Thanks," Catherine said calmly at last. "You know, when you're not playing the schoolboy Casanova, you're not so bad yourself." She slid off the wall. "Look, I've just got to go and have a word with Emma Freeman. I'm playing tennis with her and a couple of other girls at lunchtime. I won't be long."

I watched her walk away, my feelings all mixed up inside me. I was blissed out that she liked me – sort of – but I was frustrated because I wanted to push things along a lot faster. I was used to bein' in control around relationships, and somehow I didn't feel in control of this one at all. It was Catherine who was setting the pace. Still, I'd made a start. And I was convinced she'd like me even more if Dannyboy Greene wasn't coming along and sticking his nose in every five minutes. Him and his stupid love-poetry.

Catherine had left her schoolbag behind her, on the wall. I stared at it for a moment or two, turning things over in my mind. OK, so it was wrong to stick my nose into someone else's private papers. But then I wasn't an ordinary person, was I? I was a Guardian Angel and I had responsibilities. Anyway, I wanted to see what sickly romantic slush that creep Greene had been writing. I reached out, flipped open the top of Catherine's bag and pulled those mysterious papers out. My hands shaking, I unfolded the pile, and glanced through them.

They weren't love poetry. They were bills.

Unpaid bills. A whole stack of them, addressed to Catherine and her mom. Gas, water, electricity, a bill for mending the TV set, a letter from a mortgage company about the arrears. My heart thudding, I quickly totalled up the complete amount they owed. Around five hundred pounds. Jeez.

Feeling pretty agitated, I stood up and began to pace up and down. Five hundred pounds. This was serious. The time for Catherine to see sense and call in some professional help was well overdue. And it was supposed to be part of my Guardian Angelship to persuade her to do just that. But how was I going to manage it? I'd tried to persuade her once before to ask for help on the night of the disco and look where that had got me. A humungous row, and my head well and truly bitten off. If I tackled her about it now, I knew what would happen. She'd chew my head off yet again, we'd have another big row – and I could say goodbye to my chances of getting her to fall for me. All Daniel Greene would have to do was to open his arms, and Catherine would walk straight into them. And I'd be left looking like a complete and utter jerk in front of the whole school. Turned down in favour of a dork like Daniel Greene. No, I couldn't take the shame and humiliation.

Quickly I stuffed the bills back into Catherine's schoolbag. I felt like the biggest out-and-out-heel of all time. If I was a real friend, I'd be persuading her to get everything sorted out, maybe talk to Mrs B. and tell her what was going on, for starters. The old bat would know what to do, and she'd help Catherine get it together. But I knew that if I tried to persuade Lucas to do that, she'd hit the ceiling.

I said nothing about the bills to Catherine when she came back. I said nothing about the bills to Catherine for the rest of the day, which passed uneventfully, apart from Daniel Greene stealing my Reeboks when I was in the showers after games. I had to hobble around all afternoon in a gross pair of tennis shoes a size too small that Mrs B. found me in Lost Property. Humiliating, to say the least.

I wasn't looking forward to going back Up There at the end of the day either. I was bracing myself for a mega-blast in the ear from Jo-Jo for not doing anything about those bills, and I didn't have any idea how I was going to explain myself away. I felt bad enough about it as it was, without Jo-Jo goin' on at me. But, I mean, I was making headway with Catherine at last. Can you blame me for not wanting to rock the boat? Don't answer that.

Guess my luck was in though. When I got back Up There, Jo-Jo was nowhere to be seen. Instead he'd left a note for me, pinned to his cloud.

"Gotta fly, dude. Super-important business elsewhere for the next few days. Still, I guess you can cope on your own for a while. You're doin' just fine. Love and peace, J."

That made me feel even more lousy. I wasn't doing fine at all. And I sure wasn't livin' up to my responsibilities as a Guardian Angel. But the alternative made me want to spit. I couldn't just steam in and ruin my growing relationship with Catherine. Especially if it meant Daniel Greene coming off best. That was something my monumental pride just couldn't handle. So I just couldn't see any way round it.

Wednesday morning. I was late getting down to earth because Jo-Jo wasn't around to keep me on schedule, and by the time I finally materialized, I'd missed the bell, and the schoolyard was deserted. I raced down the corridor to class, cursing under my breath. With all the problems I had at the moment, I could have done without getting on the wrong side of Mrs B. today.

I was in luck. When I got to class, instead of the normal quiet, speak-and-you-die-type atmosphere that Mrs B. was so ace at enforcing, the room was in uproar. For a start, the place seemed twice as full as usual. Full of people talking with American accents, and wearing tracksuits with the Stars and Stripes on the back. I blinked. Then I sussed. It looked like the American exchange students had arrived. That cheered me up somewhat seriously. Having a few friendly countrymen (and women) to talk to could only be an excellent thing after all the problems I'd been having.

Mrs B. was running around like a mad thing with a pile of papers in her hand, trying to organize everybody. I stepped swiftly out of her way, and cast a curious eye over the new arrivals. One of the exchange babes looked especially worthy of close attention. A mane of blonde hair, long legs, big blue eyes. In fact, she looked a lot like Shelley Markowitz, my ex-girlfriend from back home.

Help.

It *was* Shelley Markowitz.

CHAPTER TEN

I was about to go into major freak-out. But before I could do so, Shelley Markowitz glanced across the room and saw me. Our eyes met. And she freaked first.

"Oh my GOD!" With a loud, hysterical scream, she passed out right in front of me, and crumpled to the floor in a quivering heap. There was a shocked silence for a second or two, and then Mrs B. and virtually everyone else in the room rushed over to her. Under cover of the noise and confusion, I hightailed it out of the room at speed.

My legs felt as if they'd turned to water as I raced down the corridor towards the boys' washroom. What the hell was going down here? As far as Shelley Markowitz was concerned, I'd been dead for the last three months. Now here I was, apparently live and well again, turning up in a school thousands of miles away in England. No wonder the poor babe had passed out. Now that I thought about it, I could vaguely remember Shelley telling me she was going on an exchange visit to the UK just before I'd kicked it, but I'd never dreamt in a billion years that she was gonna turn up at Petersfield Comp, and find me walking about as large as life. Someone Up There had goofed badly.

I flung open the washroom door with a crash. There was nobody else in there which was lucky for them, because otherwise I'd have kicked them out right away. I raced over to the mirror, stood in front of it, and stared at myself so hard, I went cross-eyed.

"C'mon, Jo-Jo, c'mon! I don't care what you're doin' or where you are, I need you!" I pleaded aloud through gritted teeth. "Where are you, you stupid hippy hologram?"

"Hey, I heard that." Jo-Jo's head materialized in the mirror, floating rather eerily on top of the reflection of my own body. "Calm down. Relax. Like, mellow out man."

"Mellow out?" I choked. "I've just sent my ex-girlfriend into screaming hysterics and you tell me to mellow out? I thought you guys were supposed to be omnipotent!"

"Minor error, man." Jo-Jo adjusted his headband, looking unconcerned. "Like, with everything we've gotta do, mistakes sometimes happen."

"Fine. Well, that's just dandy," I snapped sarcastically. "So all I have to do is to stroll back into class, and say 'Hi, Shelley. Yep, it's me, and I'm still dead, but I can live with it if you can'?"

"You're too stressed out, man." Jo-Jo shook his head reprovingly at me. "You should take up yoga. Look, we'll wipe Shelley's memory banks, OK? When she comes round, she won't know you."

"Yeah? Will that work?" I asked suspiciously.

"Hey, are you questioning the Boss Man's power here, man?"

"No, 'course not," I broke in quickly. "Sorry, it was just a bit of a shock coming face to face with her like that." A bit of a shock. That had to be the understatement of the last couple of centuries.

"Like I told you, relax," Jo-Jo said soothingly. "Everything's gonna be cool, man. The chick won't remember you. She won't remember you dated, she won't remember your family or your friends, she won't remember your name or your birthday or your favourite food. It'll be like you never existed in her life before now."

I wished I felt as confident as he did. I walked slowly over to the door, dreading the

145

moment when I had to go back into class and face Shelley Markowitz again. Then a sudden, alarming thought struck me.

"Hey, Jo-Jo, Shelley's going to be OK, isn't she? I mean, I didn't scare her so much that she…"

"She ain't joining us Up There just yet, if that's what you mean," Jo-Jo said with a grin. "Go on, get outta here. It'll be cool. Trust me."

Secretly, I wasn't convinced. I went back down the corridor to class, making contingency plans just in case Shelley recognized me again, and announced to Mrs B. and the whole class that I was supposed to be dead. As far as I could see, I had three options: (1) I could deny that I was dead at all. I was pretty sure I could pull it off – after all, I looked real enough. But that meant poor old Markowitz would probably be taken away double-quick by the men in white coats. (2) I could claim that I was the dead guy's long-lost twin brother (somewhat spookily, also called Aidan) or (3) I could get Jo-Jo to beam me back Up There pronto, and forget the whole Lucas shebang for good. Which was something I didn't want at all. No way. As I reached the classroom door, I took a deep, steadying breath. Basically I just had to bite the bullet, and hope that Jo-Jo had done his stuff.

I looked nervously through the open doorway. The first thing I saw was Shelley sitting on a chair with a glass of water in her hand, surrounded by Mrs Bradley, all the other exchange students and most of the class.

"...and I guess it was just jet-lag or something," Shelley was saying. The familiar sound of her voice sent a shiver down my backbone. "I'm OK now."

"I think perhaps you'd better go and have a lie-down." Mrs B. was fussing round her, looking pretty worried. "You don't want to overdo things on your first day."

"Really, I'm fine, Mrs Bradley," Shelley insisted with a faint smile. "I'd rather stay. I don't want to miss out on anything."

"Well, if you're sure." Mrs Bradley looked doubtful. "Come on, the rest of you, this isn't a sideshow. Get back to your seats so I can take the register. And Shelley, if you feel ill again during the day, you'd better go and see the nurse."

"OK, Mrs Bradley."

As everyone moved to sit down, I slipped into the room under cover of the noise and confusion. Unfortunately for me, I'd just got my butt inside, when Shelley glanced up and saw me again.

I went hot and cold all over as our eyes met and held for the second time. Jo-Jo had said that she wouldn't know me, right? That all her memories of me had been wiped clean away, right? So could somebody please explain to me why Shelley Markowitz was sitting there and staring at me so hard that her eyeballs were practically falling out of her head?

I froze. I would've put Plan Number Three into operation somewhat smartly if I'd been able to move. Instead I just stood there, rooted to the spot with panic, and waiting for Shelley to say "Hey, aren't you that dead guy I used to know?"

But miraculously, nothing happened. That instant spark of recognition in Shelley's eyes that had terrified the life out of me (so to speak) suddenly vanished. Although she kept on looking at me and frowning, she didn't actually say anything. No more hysterics, nothing. I breathed a sigh of relief, and bolted to an empty seat on the far side of the room. It looked like my secret was safe.

Or so I thought. Big mistake. Because all through roll-call, Shelley Markowitz kept turning round. And staring hard at yours truly. She turned round and stared at me no less than seventeen times. I counted. At first I tried to tell myself it was because she'd noticed what a particularly attractive guy I was, but I could tell it wasn't just that. She had a definite I've-seen-this-guy-somewhere-before-but-I-can't-remember-where type look on her face. I was beginning to panic somewhat seriously. Not only that, but Catherine had noticed Shelley looking at me, and she kept on turning round to stare at Shelley staring at me. By the end of roll-call, I'd been stared at so much, I was beginning to feel like an animal in a zoo.

Only one thing for it. I had to shoot off and try to see Jo-Jo again before my next class. Because if Shelley's memory really had been wiped, how come she was staring at me like any minute she was going to remember exactly who I was and go into major hysterics again? No way was I about to hang around and wait for her to announce the fact that I was deceased to the whole school. The second the bell sounded for morning class, I snatched up my books and made for the door. Jo-Jo was just gonna have to get off his cloud, and sort things out a whole lot better than he'd done so far.

"Hi there. I'm Shelley Markowitz. Could I speak to you for a moment?" I was fast, but not fast enough. I'd forgotten how determined Shelley Markowitz could be, once she'd gotten an idea into her head. She'd moved swiftly to cut me off before I could reach the safety of the corridor, and not only that, she put out a hand to grasp my sleeve with a grip of steel. So I could hardly walk away without leaving half my jacket behind. I stood trapped in helpless panic as the rest of the class negotiated their way around us. Catherine was one of the last to leave, and I noticed her looking curiously at us as she went out of the room.

"Look, I know you're going to think I'm crazy– " Shelley stared at me, screwing up the cute little nose I remembered so well. "But have we met somewhere before?"

I coughed to try and clear the huge panic-stricken lump in my throat.

"N-no. I don't think we have," I managed to squeak.

"Oh, you're American." Shelley frowned. "Funny, I kinda knew that before you even opened your mouth. Your face looks really familiar. You've never been to Cedarville, Missouri, have you?"

"No." I almost choked at the mention of our home town, absolutely certain that at any moment she was going to remember that I was pushin' up daisies in the local churchyard. "Sorry, gotta go. I'll be late for my first class."

I walked down the corridor, turned the

corner and ran like a demented rabbit back to the boys' john. There was a junior kid in there takin' a leak. I guess I must've looked pretty damn fierce because he cleared out of there with his pants half-open, and I skidded frantically across the wet floor towards the mirror.

"Jo-Jo!"

"Hey, what gives, man? I'm supposed to be elsewhere at this very moment, and my hologrammatic power's getting, like, seriously used up." Jo-Jo's face appeared in the mirror again, but so faintly I could hardly make it out. "You're going to be late for class."

"Never mind that," I hissed at him. "You said you were going to wipe Shelley's memory out."

"And so I did, brother."

"So how come she keeps on asking me if we've met before?" I hollered at him. "This girl's driving me crazy, Jo-Jo! I swear any minute now she's gonna remember that I'm history!"

"She won't remember, man. Like I told you before, everything's been wiped right out of her memory; you, your relationship, your family, everything to do with you. As far as she's concerned, Aidan Douglas Mark 1 just never, like, existed."

"So how come she—"

"The power of love, man." The hologram of Jo-Jo was fading so fast now, he was almost transparent. "Listen, dude, Shelley really dug you when you were alive and kickin', right? Not even us guys Up Here can wipe that feeling completely out of her mind."

"The power of love," I repeated slowly, my mind whirling with questions. "You mean Shelley was so sweet on me that whatever you do, you can't stop her remembering me just a tiny little bit?" But Jo-Jo had vanished, swallowed up in my own reflection.

I leaned my head against the cold glass, feeling as if someone had just punched me hard right in my middle. What Jo-Jo said had just knocked me out. So Shelley had been that sweet on me, huh? I'd never realized before how much the girl liked me. Sure, I'd known she was keen. I just hadn't sussed she was In Love. Really in love. So much in love that although the powers-that-be had tried to wipe me right out of her head, they hadn't quite succeeded. That was mind-blowing. And when I remembered the way I'd treated Shelley when I was alive, dumping her without a word of explanation, avoiding her calls, I felt horribly cold inside.

"You stupid, no-brained bighead." I stared contemptuously at my reflection in the mirror. For once I wasn't happy with what I saw. "You deserved everything you got, you arrogant ratface."

Suddenly, as if a bright light had switched itself on inside my mind, I realised just what a jerk I'd been when I was alive. A conceited, stupid, thick-headed creep. Someone who'd spent his time trampling over people to get whatever he wanted, without caring what they were thinking and feeling inside. OK, so I hadn't realized that Shelley was so crazily in love with me, but hey, I should have known. If I'd thought less about myself and more about other people when I was live and kickin', I might have got on a whole lot better. I'd been a stupid bighead with an outsize ego and a tiny brain. And I hadn't improved none now that I was dead.

I was fifteen minutes late for chemistry class, and Baxter gave me a hundred lines and about a billion test-tubes to wash. The morning was going from bad to triple-bad. Unfortunately for me, Shelley Markowitz had joined the group, and every time I looked at her, it reminded me just how badly I'd treated her all those months ago. I sat miserably in class on my own, feeling more lonely than I'd ever done before, dead or alive, and not listening to a word of Baxter droning on. Just going over and over in my head the unpleasant truths I'd discovered about myself.

If anybody had asked me a week ago, I'd have boasted that I knew everything there was to know about girls. If there'd been a Babeology exam, I'd have been pretty damn confident about scoring straight A's all-round, in theory, practical and oral. I thought I knew it all. And now I was finding out I knew zilch. Not only had I treated Shelley like dirt when the only crime she'd committed was to fall in love with me, but I'd also expected Catherine to be a complete walkover. To come running when I snapped my fingers, and be grateful I'd bothered to take any notice of her. And when she wouldn't, I just hadn't been able to take it. There'd been other girls too, when I was alive. Girls I'd treated with casual disdain because, well, there'd always be another one waiting round the corner who wouldn't be able to resist me. Well, I sure hadn't turned out to be as irresistible as I thought I was. At the moment I didn't even *like* myself very much.

At recess, after I'd finished washing my billionth test-tube, I went right to the back of the schoolyard behind the kitchen bins, to be on my own. There was so much going round in my head all at once, it hurt. First up, I had some crazy idea about trying to apologize to Shelley for the way I'd treated her. I was desperate to put things right somehow, but I hadn't quite worked out how I could apologize for something she wouldn't even remember had happened. Second, I wanted to sort out my real feelings for Catherine. To stop messing around, to face up to the truth and to be honest with myself. Because I didn't think I'd ever been really honest with myself in life or death before. I slumped down on to the damp grass and put my head in my hands. How come everything had gone wrong on me like this?

I'd been real pleased with myself when I was alive. Smug. Cocky. Stupid. Thinking I was the World's Number One Gift to Girls, and not caring about anyone but myself. Walking all over other people's feelings, and carrying an ego around with me the size of Alaska. Thinking that because I was good-looking and smart and funny, I could treat girls whatever way I wanted. And what had I ever done to deserve the easy life I'd had? I'll tell ya – nothing. I'd never had any major problems, never had to struggle through poverty or bereavement or my parents divorcing. I'd had everything most guys could ever want, and I'd never had to work to get it either. There was one thing I knew for sure. Catherine Lucas had more guts in her little finger than I had in the whole of my miserable body. I buried my face in my hands. If only I could go back in time, I'd make pretty sure that things were different, now that I realised what a jerk I'd been. But I couldn't go back. I'd had my shot, and I'd blown it. And you know somethin'? I'd been such a no-brained butthead when I was alive, I was beginning to wonder how I'd ever got in Up There after all.

"Aidan?" The sound of Catherine's voice startled me. I glanced up. "Aidan." She was standing staring at me with wide eyes. "You're crying."

"I'm what?" Bewildered, I touched my face. It was wet. I was crying, and I hadn't even realized. "Er, no, I'm not." Quickly I dragged my sleeve across my eyes. "My eyes were watering a bit, that's all. Guess I'm just not used to the cold weather here."

"It's June," Catherine said softly.

"Yeah? Feels like the middle of winter to me." I got to my feet, trying to look unconcerned. I'd never cried in front of a girl before, and the sympathy in Catherine's eyes was cracking me up inside. A jerk like yours truly didn't deserve to be sympathized with. Cue swift change of subject. "Did you want something?"

"Well, no." For once it was Catherine who looked embarrassed. "You seemed pretty miserable in chemistry class, so I thought I'd come and check you were OK…" Her voice died away.

"Yeah, I'm OK." Or I would be when I'd sorted myself out, and made up for all the crass mistakes I'd made over the last fourteen and a bit years. Welcome to the world premiere of the new, honest, no-more-playing-games-type Aidan Douglas. OK, so it was too late for me to live my life differently now, but even though I was dead, maybe I could still change. And I could start by forgetting my own gigantic ego for once, and doing something I should have done straightaway yesterday. Which was making a determined attempt to sort out Catherine's financial problems, whatever the consequences. I breathed hard, and took the plunge.

"Catherine, I know about those bills you've got in your bag."

The sympathy in her eyes vanished like snow in the sun.

"What?"

"I said, I know about those unpaid bills. Don't get mad. Just hear me out."

Too late. The colour was already draining from Catherine's face.

"You looked in my bag?" She spat the words out at me as if they were bullets. "How dare you!"

"Catherine, just give me a chance, willya?" I said pleadingly. "Look, I tried to talk you into doin' something about this once before, and you blew me out. But I'm not going to give up. You and your mom are in a bad way, sure, but you can get some help, if you'd only ask."

It looked like my words were falling on deaf ears. Catherine had spun round on her heel, and was walking away. Determinedly I chased after her.

"I bet your mom doesn't know about those bills, right?" I grabbed her arm, and pulled her round to face me. "That's why you carry them round in your schoolbag, isn't it?"

She tried to yank herself away from me but I held her fast.

"Listen to me, Cath! I shouldn't have looked in your bag, I know but–"

"No, you shouldn't!" Catherine was very pale, and I was upset to see that she was fighting to stop the tears in her eyes from falling. "I told you before, I can cope! Why d'you have to keep on sticking your nose in?"

"Because I care about you, you stubborn idiot!" I said softly. "Look, Catherine, I want to help. But I can't do this thing for you. You've got to make up your mind to do it yourself. It ain't weak to admit you can't cope on your own, you know. Nobody could." I stared deep into her eyes, willing her to make a decision. "Are you going to carry on struggling and going under, or are you going to swallow a bit of pride, and let people who care about you help you? All you'd have to do is talk to Mrs B. for starters. She'd know what to do."

I was getting precisely nowhere. Catherine simply pulled her arm free of my grasp, and half-ran, half-walked away. I watched her go, feeling sick and miserable inside. I'd only done what I had to do. But in the process I'd destroyed the closeness that had slowly been building up between us for the last couple of days. I closed my eyes and drew a long, shaky breath. Catherine was probably hating my guts right at this very minute. Maybe she'd even gone straight to Daniel Greene for comfort... My heart twisted with pain at the thought, but I fought it down. The new-style Aidan Douglas could cope with rejection and humiliation in the line of duty. And now that I'd made a start, I wasn't going to give up until I'd sorted out Catherine's problems for good. I'd have another word with her at lunchtime when she might have calmed down a bit.

I didn't get the chance. When I trailed back into class after recess, Catherine was nowhere to be seen. She wasn't in history or English Lit. either. I began to get seriously alarmed. She hadn't run off and done anything stupid, had she?

"Dan?" Half out of my mind with worry, I cornered Daniel in the canteen at lunchtime. "Have you seen Catherine? She wasn't in any of our classes after recess."

"I asked Mrs Bradley, and she said Catherine had gone home." Daniel looked just as worried as I was. "I suppose she wasn't feeling well or something."

And we all knew whose fault that was.

"Oh." I raked a hand through my hair, feeling guiltier than guilty. Couldn't I do anything right? Jeez, once I'd thought I was the smartest guy in the world. Now I was beginning to realize just how bone-headed I really was.

What with worrying about Catherine, and trying to dodge Shelley Markowitz, who was still following me around with that gleam of recognition in her eye, I had a pretty bad day. Jo-Jo was still absent on his super-important business, so I couldn't even ask him to let me in on what had happened to Catherine after she'd left me. I was just gonna have to wait until tomorrow, and then try to sort everything out as best as I could. But it was the waiting that was killing me. I couldn't bear the thought of Catherine sitting miserably at home, hating me.

The following day, things went from bad to mega-bad. Catherine didn't turn up for class again, and I was somewhat seriously off my head with anxiety. I needed to see her, to talk things through with her for her sake as well as my own, and she just wasn't around. I'd tried asking Mrs B. if she knew anything, but she'd just told me not to worry. Huh. Tell the sun not to shine.

By the end of the day, I'd made up my mind. I was going to go and see Catherine, and find out what was going on. I knew that tonight was one of her shifts at the Bigshot Burger Bar, so I decided to turn up there. I wasn't supposed to leave the school and go off on my own without getting permission from Jo-Jo, but he wasn't around, and anyway, I figured that this was an emergency.

Somebody else had had the same idea. As I walked up the street towards the Bigshot Burger Bar, the first thing I saw was Daniel Greene coming towards me from the opposite direction. We both stopped and looked at each other warily.

"I just wanted to see how Catherine was," we both said at exactly the same moment, and then we grinned at each other.

"You've been worried, huh?" I said as we went over to the grimy windows of the café together, and peered inside. "Me too."

"Do you think she's ill?" Daniel asked me anxiously. "I would've gone to her house first, but I wasn't sure of her address."

"Nah, I don't reckon she's sick," I said slowly. Sick of me, maybe, but not actually ill. "I just think she's got a few other problems."

"Well, it doesn't look like she's arrived yet." Daniel nodded at the cafe door. "Want to go and wait inside?"

"Are you kidding? I'd rather spend time sittin' on a dungheap." I stuck my hands in my pockets, and leaned against the wall. There were a few things I needed to get straight with Daniel Greene right away, and the Bigshot Burger Bar wasn't the kind of place I wanted to do it. "Dan, about Catherine."

162

"What about her?"

I searched for the right words to say what I wanted to say.

"I just wanted to tell you – well, I'm not goin' to be chasing after Catherine any more. I mean, I don't want to date her now. I just thought you ought to know."

"What?" Daniel looked as if he couldn't believe his ears. "Why? I thought you fancied her like crazy."

I was silent for a moment or two. What could I say? That I'd finally realized what a spoilt, selfish brat I was, goin' all-out to make Catherine fall in love with a guy who was dead? That I'd only set out to make her fall for me because I couldn't stand being turned down by a babe, and I didn't want to be humiliated in front of the whole school? That right from the start of my relationship with Catherine, all I'd done was think about myself and my own feelings for most of the time, just the same as I'd done when I was alive? That Catherine Lucas deserved more, much more, than a jerk like me (and a dead jerk at that) could give her? No. I couldn't tell Daniel Greene any of those things.

"Look, forget it, OK?" I swallowed down a painful lump that was blocking my throat. "Just ask the girl to the prom tomorrow night, willya, and get something moving between the two of you."

Daniel was still staring at me, bewildered.

"So have you gone off Catherine or what?"

Gone off her? Gone off the most damn interesting babe I'd ever met in my whole life or death? No. I hadn't gone off Catherine Lucas. In fact…

"Catherine!" Daniel's face suddenly lit up, and he started waving and yelling over my shoulder. I looked round and my heart missed a beat. Catherine was coming up the street towards us. And she looked OK. A bit pale maybe, but she was all in one piece. A wave of relief washed over me.

"What're you two doing here?" Catherine's eyes widened at the sight of us. She threw me a wary look, but she didn't seem too upset to see me. Which made me feel a lot better.

"We were worried about you," Daniel said. "Are you OK?"

"I'm fine," Catherine said briskly. She walked purposefully up to the burger bar door and flung it open. "Come on then. I want to get this over with."

"Get what over with?" I asked, bemused.

"You'll see." She practically frogmarched us

into the café, and then slammed the door shut behind us without another word. I glanced around. Nothing had improved since the last time I was there. In fact, it looked as if a couple of extra layers of grease and dirt had settled on everything in the meantime. Ratface Mr Burton was behind the counter as usual, frying burgers, and lookig as if he was hot favourite for the title of Greaseball of The Year. There was a gang of bored-looking juveniles draped all over the jukebox, a few trucker-types at various tables and right over in the corner, without his band of merry men for once, sat Blond Creepo. He of the coffee-covered crotch. My stomach turned at the sight of him.

"Don't sit down by the way," Catherine said under her breath. "We're not staying." It was then that I noticed that light-of-battle gleam in her eyes. Something else struck me too.

"Hey, where's your uniform? Aren't you supposed to be working tonight?"

Catherine didn't answer. She left Daniel and me standing by the door, and walked over to the counter where Burton was frying his salmonella specials.

"You're late again, Lucas," he growled with that especially charming manner of his. "That's–"

"A quid off my wages. I know," Catherine cut in calmly. "That's why I made sure you'd paid me up to date before I did this."

Burton stared at her.

"Did what?"

"This." Calmly Catherine picked up a huge squeezy bottle of tomato relish that stood on the counter, and aimed it straight at Burton's eye. Red gloop flew out in a rush, and hit its target full on.

"Yee-ah!" His face dripping, Burton danced about wildly behind his griddle. "I can't see! You've blinded me!" As he scrabbled for the dirty towel hanging on the hook behind him, the whole of the café watched in silence with their mouths hanging open, including me and Daniel.

"OK, you lot. Listen carefully." Catherine walked into the middle of the floor and stood with her hands on her hips, looking around her. I was mesmerized, along with everybody else. She was truly wonderful when she got going. "I think you've got a right to know that you take your life in your hands when you eat here. Number one, Burton gets his burgers really cheap because they're miles past their sell-by date. Number two, the potatoes he uses for the chips are usually mouldy and number three, he

166

never ever washes his hands after he's been to the loo." One of the truckers, who'd just been about to take a big bite out of his burger in a bun, turned somewhat green, and dropped it back on to his plate. "And there're rats in the storeroom back there where he keeps all the food."

"Oi!" Burger Burton was trying to wipe his face with the towel and wave his fist at Catherine at the same time. "I'll sue you for this. That's slander, that is!"

Catherine ignored him. She'd spun slowly round to stare at Blond Creepo in the corner.

"You and I have got some unfinished business as well. Haven't we?" She advanced across the cafe, the relish bottle held in her hand like a Smith and Wesson and pointing straight in Blond Creepo's direction. BC didn't seem able to move. He was sitting there with his eyes popping out of his head and a forkful of french fries suspended in mid-air. Catherine paused inches in front of him, and fixed him with a steely glare.

"I've had to put up with insult after insult from you and your mates for the last few months," she snapped at him. "I think it's about time you apologized, don't you?"

Daniel and I watched spellbound as BC

opened and closed his mouth several times. At last a sound came out.

"Sorry," he squeaked.

"Thank you." Catherine slammed the plastic bottle down onto the table with a force that nearly made everybody jump out of their skins. "And next time, think before you open that big mouth of yours." Then, with her head held high, she swept across the café and over to the door. As she went past Daniel and me, she winked at us. And then I knew.

I was in love with her. It wasn't just 'flu or feeling sorry for her or not wanting to lose out to Daniel Greene. At last the new-style, honest-to-goodness Aidan Douglas could finally admit it to himself. *I was in love with Catherine Lucas.*

I'd never been in love in my life (or death) before. And it felt mind-blowing.

In a daze I followed Daniel and Catherine out of the burger bar. Dan was talking excitedly, telling Catherine how brilliant she'd been in there, but I couldn't speak. My mind was stuck in one groove. I'm in love, I'm in love, I'm in love...

"What made you do it though, Cath?" Daniel was asking curiously. "I thought you really needed that job."

"I did." Catherine glanced over and smiled at me. She wasn't as gorgeous as Shelley Markowitz and her spots hadn't cleared up either. But right at that moment I thought she was the most beautiful babe in the whole world. "Until Aidan stuck his big, fat, interfering nose in."

"Me?" I looked dreamily at her. "What did I do?"

"You had a go at me the other day." Catherine looked me straight in the eyes. "You told me I was a stubborn idiot. You were right."

My mouth fell open in amazement.

"You mean…"

"Yeah. You said I ought to ask for help, and deep down I knew you were right. So I thought about it, and I decided to go and see Mrs Bradley." Catherine managed a smile, but I could see that she wasn't that far away from tears. "She was so nice. She arranged for me to see someone at Social Services, and some people from a couple of charities for the disabled. That's why I wasn't at school today."

"So are you going to get any help or not?" It was Daniel who asked the question. I was still too speechless with shock to say anything.

"Well, Social Services aren't exactly throwing money at us, but they're going to sort out all the benefits we're entitled to. Oh, and there might be a chance of us getting a home help." There was an unmistakable note of relief in Catherine's voice. "And they're going to contact my father about paying maintenance." She looked over at me again, and my heart quivered. "Thanks, Aidan," she said simply. "I'd never have done it without you."

"That's OK." I felt as if I was floating on air. I could have stood there and watched her smile at me all night. But Daniel soon put a stop to that.

"I'll walk you home, Cath."

"OK." Catherine's gaze held mine. "You're coming to the prom tomorrow night, aren't you, Aidan?"

"Try and stop me." I could hardly believe what was happening to me. Aidan Douglas, the cynical, the hard-boiled, the romeo, the dater of many girls simultaneously, was in love. *In love.* Jeez. Life was pretty damn good. "I'll see you there."

I watched Daniel and Catherine walk away together, and then I wandered dreamily down the street in the opposite direction, making plans. Maybe I'd been a bit too hasty telling Daniel I wasn't gonna try and date Catherine any more. I mean, now that I'd realized I was in love with the girl, things were different. Feeling happier than I'd ever done before, I gazed into the shops as I drifted by, not seeing anything in front of my eyes except Catherine's face. I was sure going to enjoy being in love. Hey, I was enjoying it already.

I stared blissfully into the window of a clothes shop as I went past. One of the mannequins was dressed as a hippy, and it was moving. One of the shop dummies was moving! With a screech of terror I leapt backwards. Then I saw Jo-Jo grinning and waving at me through the glass.

"Hey, man! Over here!"

"You're going to give me a heart attack if you keep appearing out of nowhere like that," I hissed, checking over my shoulder to make sure nobody else was around. "What're you doing here?"

Jo-Jo cocked an eyebrow at me.

"More to the point, man, what're *you* doin' here? You're not supposed to go wanderin' off without permission, remember?"

"Yeah, I know," I said hastily, "But,"

"Hey, never mind that, man. I forgive you." Jo-Jo was looking as excited as if he'd just found Jimi Hendrix at long last. "I mean, you've done it, haven't you? At long last you've finally got Catherine Lucas's life back on track." He beamed at me through the plate-glass. "Mission accomplished, brother. Ain't no need for you to hang around down here for a minute longer. Time to come back Home. For good."

CHAPTER ELEVEN

The school hall was looking pretty spectacular. There was a big banner across the stage saying "Welcome to Prom Night", and there were loads of red, white and blue balloons and streamers, as well as the ol' Stars and Stripes, hanging everywhere. Mrs B. and a couple of the other teachers were running around like mad things at one end of the hall, handing out cheeseburgers and cokes to the hungry hordes, and they'd hired a DJ who was a Cockney, but who was pretending to have an American accent. A pretty bad American accent. Guess you lot were getting your revenge at last for Dick Van Dyke in Mary Poppins.

So what was little ol' me doin' there at all after Jo-Jo had told me that my time on earth was finito? I'd spent the whole day nagging and pleading with Jo-Jo to let me go back down to earth one more time, and after mucho grovelling, I'd finally started to get somewhere.

"Look, man, there ain't no point in going

back to say goodbye," Jo-Jo had explained patiently to me for the ten thousandth time. "The second you're, like, back Up Here, they won't remember you any more."

"I know that." But I was desperate. I had to see Catherine for one last time. I didn't care how I did it. I didn't even care if the Powers-That-Be Up Here knew that I'd fallen for her. And I guess they had to know. I mean, they knew everything, right? "Jo-Jo, this is something I've just gotta do. Look, I did OK so far, didn't I?"

"You did triple-OK." Jo-Jo beamed proudly at me. "Catherine Lucas is going to be fine now, thanks to you."

"So how about pushin' a bit of reward my way?"

Jo-Jo looked at me in silence for about five minutes with his head on one side.

"Well, OK. You can go to the prom tonight, and that's all, man," he said at last. I felt like leaping on him and hugging him. "But don't get too carried away. You'll be leavin' express at midnight."

Midnight. I stood in the middle of the hall, surrounded by a thumping beat, and glanced at the clock hung over the stage where the fake American DJ was doin' his stuff. 10.20 p.m. I'd spent the first hour or two dancing with Emma Freeman and some of the other babes in our class, and saying my goodbyes. Only one hour and forty minutes to go. I was beginning to feel like Cinderella.

The place was jammed to the roof with kids, and it was almost impossible to move in any direction except by shuffling along like a tortoise with a limp. I hadn't managed to meet up with Daniel and Catherine yet, but I knew they'd be around somewhere. And anyway, I wanted to leave my goodbye to Catherine until last. For obvious reasons. Besides, I had a couple of other people to see first. So I went down to the refreshments table at the end of the hall, and queued up for a coke.

"Hiya, Mrs B. A coke please." I winked at her as I got to the front of the queue. "Betcha've got a crate of Budweisers back there for the teachers."

"Actually we've got a couple of dozen bottles of Wild Turkey," Mrs B. snapped back with a straight face. "I hope you've got a good explanation for why you weren't at school today, Mr Douglas."

"That's what I wanted to tell you." I managed a smile, but even saying the words tore me apart inside. "I'm leavin' today."

"What?" Surprised, Mrs B. looked up at me and almost poured coke all over the table. "You mean you're going back to America? That's rather sudden, isn't it?"

"I'm going home, yeah," I said evasively, swallowing down a hard lump in my throat. "Thanks for everything, Mrs B."

"I think it's me who ought to be thanking you," Mrs Bradley said with a smile.

"What for?"

"For persuading Catherine Lucas to come and tell me her problems. I've had a feeling for quite a while that there was something wrong, but Catherine just wouldn't admit it." Mrs. B. looked at me thoughtfully. "You're quite a remarkable young man, you know, Mr Douglas."

"Yeah, well, I guess the jury's still out on that one." I leaned across the table and gave her a quick kiss on the cheek. "I'll see you around sometime."

She turned pink. I guess I'd got quite fond of the hawk-eyed Teacher from Hell.

"Have a good trip, Mr Douglas."

"Thanks." I picked up my drink. "How much do I owe you?"

"On the house." She winked at me, and turned to the next person in the queue. "Yes? Come on, I haven't got all day."

Clutching my drink, I plunged back into the seething mass of kids shakin' it all about on the dance floor. The clock said 10.40. An hour and twenty minutes to go. Had to get a move on, if I wanted to spend my last hour on earth with Catherine. Time for Farewell Number Two on my list.

There was a little group of exchange students standing at the side of the hall. Shelley Markowitz was one of them. I headed towards her.

"Hi, Shelley." She was looking beautiful in a red dress with black lace sleeves. I'd seen her wear it once before when I'd taken her to a party back home in Cedarville. My eyes began to prickle, and I blinked hastily. "Can I talk to you for a minute?"

"Sure." She smiled at me, and I wondered how I could ever have treated her the way I had. What a bonehead I'd been. At least I'd realized it, at long last.

"I, er, just wanted to tell you that I'm going home. Tonight."

"Back to the good ol' US of A? Well, give it my love." She was frowning again now with that look in her eyes that always made my heart sink. "Where did you say you came from, by the say?"

"I didn't," I said softly. "It's just a tiny little town on the West Coast. You wouldn't know it."

"Well, maybe we'll see each other again when I come home?" Shelley suggested, fluttering her eyelashes at me.

"Sure." But I hoped for her sake that that wouldn't be for a very long time. "Look, Shelley," now for the difficult bit. "I just wanted to say, well, I think you're a great girl."

Shelley looked taken aback, but she rallied fast. "Why thanks very much, er, sorry – what did you say your name was?"

"Aidan." I looked straight at her. "Aidan There was that very slight flicker in her eyes again, and then it was gone.

"Well, have a good trip, Aidan." She leaned over and gave me a friendly hug. I held her close for a second or two, and smelt her familiar perfume.

"Take care of yourself," I said softly, as I let her go. "Have a great life."

11.00 p.m. Time to find Daniel and Catherine. I drained the last drops of my coke, and took a deep breath. In exactly one hour precisely I'd be beaming back Up There and leaving behind a whole group of people I'd got to caring about. Catherine Lucas most of all.

The hall was so stuffed with people, it took me almost fifteen minutes to find them. I saw Daniel first, standing talking to some of the other guys in our class. I glanced around, but I couldn't see Catherine. I guess she'd gone to the washroom or something. Which suited me fine. I wanted to corner her and say my goodbyes to her alone.

"Hey, Dan." I tapped him lightly on the shoulder. "Got a minute? I just wanted to say goodbye."

"Goodbye?" Daniel stared at me, bewildered. "What, you mean your leaving? Is that why you weren't at school today?"

"Yep. I'm going tonight." I held out my hand. "Been nice knowin' you, Dan." I meant it too. I guess I was gonna miss the big jerk quite a bit. And I knew he'd be a good friend Catherine could rely on when I was gone. Who knows, they might even get it together in the romance department too.

"It's a bit sudden, isn't it?" Daniel frowned. "I thought you were here for the year."

"Yeah, well, things have turned out a bit differently than I thought." You could say that again. "Look, Dan, about Catherine. I hope things work out between the two of you. I really mean that."

"Thanks, mate." Daniel held out his hand and we shook. "I'll tell her you've gone. She's going to be really disappointed she didn't get a chance to say goodbye."

"What?" I said, bewildered. "What do you mean? She's round here somewhere, isn't she?"

To my horror, Daniel shook his head.

"No, she couldn't make it in the end. Her mum's got a cold. Nothing serious, but Cath didn't want to leave her – Aidan!"

I'd raced away from him and across the hall, trampling a few dancers underfoot, and elbowing several more out of my way.

"Be lucky, Dan!" I called back over my shoulder.

The clock said 11.16. And Catherine's home was about a forty-minute walk away. I could catch a bus, except I didn't have a clue which one to get. No, I couldn't afford any slip-ups. I was gonna have to run like Carl Lewis, and then some, to make it to say goodbye before midnight.

I torpedoed out of school and down the road faster than I'd ever moved in life or death before. Right at this moment there was nothing more important than that I should get to Catherine in time to say goodbye. I had to see her one more time before I left. The last time.

I followed the same route I'd taken almost

three weeks ago when I'd trailed Catherine home from school that first day. As I pounded along the sidewalk, I thought about how much I'd changed, as well as Catherine, over the past weeks. I guess I'd learned a lot about myself, most of it not very pleasant. Still, better late than never.

When I got to the Lucases' place, I threw open the gate and staggered up the path, wheezing heavily. I wasn't wearing a watch, so I didn't know what the time was. I could have fifteen minutes left on earth or fifteen seconds. I had to be quick.

The lounge curtains were drawn, but there was a faint lamplight shining behind them. Breathing hard, I knocked softly on the door. If Catherine's mom was asleep, I didn't want to wake her.

I waited. No answer. Feeling more desperate with every second that ticked away, I knocked a little more loudly. Still silence. And then I heard the sound of footsteps in the hall. A second later the door swung open a chink.

"Aidan!" Catherine stared at me in amazement. "What're you doing here?"

"I had to see you," I wheezed. She pulled the door open wider and I limped painfully into the hallway. All those days lying around trying to look beatific had left me seriously unfit. "Daniel told me about your mom. How is she?"

"Not too bad." Putting her finger to her lips, Catherine led me to the lounge doorway, and nodded across the room. Her mom was asleep in the bed. "Keep your voice down though, will you? She's only just gone off."

"OK." I glanced at the ancient clock on the mantelpiece. 11.37. Boy, I'd covered that distance in a time an Olympic athlete would've been proud of. Twenty-three minutes to go.

"Did I tell you we're getting the house decorated in a few weeks' time?" Catherine whispered to me, looking round the dilapidated living-room. "That charity I was telling you about have got a team of volunteers who do it for free."

"Great." My heart ached as I looked down at her. Only twenty-two minutes left and counting. "I'm glad everything worked out OK."

"And I'm glad you made me see what a stupid, pig-headed idiot I was." Catherine smiled shyly at me. "Mum had been trying to persuade me for ages that we needed some outside help, but I thought I could manage on my own."

"Nobody could have coped with all that

alone." I felt as if I was falling into the deep. sea-coloured pools of her eyes. "But you made a better job of it than most kids would've done. You're a pretty amazing person."

"Flattery will get you everywhere." Was Catherine moving closer to me, or was it just a trick of the dim lamplight? "I just wanted to say if you still want to go out with me, I'd like to go out with you. Very much."

"You mean...?" I was so shocked, I could hardly speak.

"I know, I know. I told you you weren't my type." Catherine was blushing. "OK, so I lied a bit. I always thought you were gorgeous. But I honestly didn't *like* you very much at first."

"You like me *now*?" Joy flooded through me like a beam of light. "You really want to date me?"

"If you still want to."

"You know I do!" And then it struck me. The sheer cruelty of the situation. I was leaving earth forever in precisely nineteen minutes. Leaving behind the girl I loved. She was finally telling me that she cared for me, and I'd come to say goodbye. I turned cold inside.

"Aidan?" Catherine put her hand on my arm. "What's the matter? You've gone as white as a sheet."

"Nothing." I made my decision as fast as lightning. I wasn't going to tell Catherine I was leaving. I loved her, and I didn't want to hurt her. I'd just have to shoulder the suffering for the both of us. It was the least I could do. "Look, Catherine," I said urgently. "I just want you to know – I've never felt this way about any other girl before."

"Oh, go on." Catherine looked up at me teasingly. "I bet you've said that to all your girls."

"Yeah, I have actually," I admitted with a grin. "But I never meant it before now. You know somethin'? You made me see what a jerk I am."

"You make yourself sound irresistible." Catherine put her hands on her hips and stared at me teasingly. "I'm not sure I want to go out with you after all."

"Hey, you can't get out of it now." I glanced at the clock again. 11.47. Thirteen minutes to go and I hadn't even kissed the girl yet. I put out my hand to pull her closer to me, and then I froze. My hand was transparent, and fading away even as I stared at it in horror.

"Cath," I gasped, "is that clock over there tellin' the right time?"

"What?" Taken aback, she glanced round.

"No, it's about ten minutes slow. Why?"

Ten minutes slow. That meant it was 11.57. Three minutes to midnight and counting. Frantically I reached out and pulled Catherine into my arms.

"I love you," I said urgently. "Don't ever forget that."

Our lips touched, but it was already too late. Even while we were kissing for the very last time, I could feel some great force jerking me away. We broke apart, and I saw the bright white light at my feet beginning to swirl upwards.

"Catherine!" I yelled despairingly, feeling as if my heart was going to burst with misery. But her face had gone blank, and she'd already turned away. I guessed that she couldn't see me or hear me any longer, and my throat swelled up with tears. Aching with longing, I watched her sit down in an armchair and stare at the bright bars of the fire. As the light swirled up around my waist, Catherine's mom sat up in the bed across the room.

"Catherine? Are you all right?"

Catherine started.

"Sorry, Mum. Did I wake you up? I was just sitting her thinking."

"What about, love?"

As the light floated upwards and around my shoulders, I saw Catherine's face soften into a smile.

"Oh, just about someone I used to know."

She remembered me. Just like Shelley, I'd left a tiny bit of myself in her mind. A faint memory, but one she'd never forget. I took a last, long look at her face before the white light swallowed me. She'd remember me, vaguely at least, for the rest of her life. And I'd sure never forget her.

"Hey, all right, brother?" Jo-Jo's voice was gentle in my ear, but I couldn't see him. Then I realized that the bright light had vanished, and I couldn't see because my eyes were blurred with tears.

"Fine." Quickly I dashed my sleeve across my face, and looked around me. I was back Up There. "So that's that then."

"Yep. And you've done a great job, kid. Congratulations."

"Thanks." I coughed a few times to try and get rid of the hard lump of misery in my throat. C'mon, Aidan, I told myself sternly, you might have had to leave, but at least you know Catherine's going to be OK. That was the most important thing.

"The Boss Man is pretty blissed about this."

Jo-Jo was looking at me in a way I didn't understand. Kinda meaningfully. "He reckons you did real well. Considering."

There was an enigmatic note in Jo-Jo's voice that puzzled me.

"Considering what?"

"Considerin' the kinda guy you were when this whole thing started." Jo-Jo nodded thoughtfully at me. "You've changed, man. For the better."

"Yeah, I know." A sudden thought was striking me somewhat seriously. I'd been sent down to earth to help Catherine, sure, but I was beginning to wonder if the Boss Man had chosen me to be her Guardian Angel because he'd had some kind of lesson in mind for yours truly, the original bighead. If that was the case, then it sure explained a lot. I shot Jo-Jo a curious stare. "Maybe that was all part of the Boss Man's masterplan."

"Hey, don't ask me, kid." Jo-Jo shrugged, and looked innocent. "I'm just the messenger boy."

I ran my hand through my hair, my mind buzzing with questions that I knew I wouldn't get any answers to. I was pretty sure I'd hit on the truth. I'd been – what had Catherine called me? – a prat, and the Boss had given me a second chance to put myself right. And I was pretty damn grateful for that. If only I'd had the sense to realize what an idiot I was when I was alive. I had to fight back a sudden surge of emotion that overwhelmed me, and threatened to end in tears. Still, I guess it was better late than never.

"So what happens now?" I asked quietly.

"You take a break, man," Jo-Jo said with a smile. "You've earned it. And, hey, you can spend some time practising that beatific look you ain't quite got the hang of yet."

"Sure." I didn't think I was going to have many problems being beatific from now on. All I had to think about was how I'd finally fallen in love for the first time ever, and a big, beatific smile would spread right over my face. OK, so Catherine and I couldn't be together, but nobody could take that feeling away from me. Pretty damn good, this love thing, isn't it? I just wish I'd discovered it sooner.

"Hey, Jo-Jo." I turned to the hippy and grinned cheekily at him. "Don't I get a prize or a reward or somethin' for wrapping up the Lucas case?"

"What did you have in mind, man?"

"How about if you get rid of that gross purple headband for starters?" I suggested airily. "That'd be reward enough for me."

Jo-Jo looked injured.

"This headband was at Woodstock with me, man."

"Pity you didn't leave it there."

"That's the trouble with you Nineties kids, man. You've got no, like, soul."

"We may not have any soul, Jo-Jo, but we've got *taste*. Take my advice, dude. Ditch the headband."

We glared at each other for a second or two, and then we both started to laugh.

In a way, it was good to be home.